Toni Harks has been crafting stories across various genres for many years, with a particular passion for fiction and comedy. Now, the time has come to share these stories through publishing. The debut release, *The Irish invincible,* is just the beginning, with many more to follow.

To my beloved children, Tyler and Hannah.

I am endlessly proud of the incredible people you are becoming. Your hard work, kindness, and boundless curiosity inspire me every day. May you always chase your dreams with courage and never forget how deeply you are loved.

Toni Harks

THE IRISH INVINCIBLE

AUSTIN MACAULEY PUBLISHERS
LONDON · CAMBRIDGE · NEW YORK · SHARJAH

Copyright © Toni Harks 2025

The right of Toni Harks to be identified as the author of this work has been asserted by the author in accordance with sections 77 and 78 of the Copyright, Designs and Patents Act 1988.

All rights reserved. No part of this publication may be reproduced, stored in a retrieval system, or transmitted in any form or by any means, electronic, mechanical, photocopying, recording, or otherwise, without the prior permission of the publishers.

Any person who commits any unauthorised act in relation to this publication may be liable to criminal prosecution and civil claims for damages.

This is a work of fiction. Names, characters, businesses, places, events, locales, and incidents are either the products of the author's imagination or used in a fictitious manner. Any resemblance to actual persons, living or dead, or actual events is purely coincidental.

A CIP catalogue record for this title is available from the British Library.

ISBN 9781037102158 (Paperback)
ISBN 9781037102172 (ePub e-book)
ISBN 9781037102165 (Audiobook)

www.austinmacauley.com

First Published 2025
Austin Macauley Publishers Ltd®
1 Canada Square
Canary Wharf
London
E14 5AA

To my wife, Monica. Your love of books and keen eye for storytelling have been an incredible gift to me. Your thoughtful perspective and insightful suggestions have helped shape my work in ways I couldn't have done alone. Your support, patience, and belief in me mean everything, and I'm endlessly grateful for your guidance and encouragement on this journey.

Chapter One

The bus ride from Tyrone to Dublin is long and winding, snaking its way through the hills and valleys Erin has known all her life. Outside the window, fields stretch in an endless quilt of green, dotted with sheep and lined by low stone walls.

She watches as the familiar countryside blurs by, her fingers tightening around the strap of her bag. Though she is in her 20s, she'd rarely ventured outside her county, let alone Northern Ireland. This trip felt monumental.

She is leaving behind the only life she has ever known, one where everyone knew each other, where the world felt close and predictable. She told herself she wanted more than that, but now, on the road to a new beginning, she finds herself flooded with doubt.

Her mother had given her an extra-long hug at the bus stop, wrapping her in arms that still seemed protective even though Erin towered over her mother with her tall frame and athletic build. Her father had offered a few gruff words of encouragement, though Erin had seen the glint of worry in his eyes.

As the bus pulled away, she felt a pang of homesickness hit her so strongly it almost left her breathless. For a moment, she'd even entertained the thought of calling out for the driver to stop, to let her off right there. It is only a few miles down the road, so she can walk back to her parents, and her quiet and familiar life.

But she doesn't. Instead, she grits her teeth and stares out at the passing hills, forcing herself to stay on this path.

The city lights are still hours away, and Erin fills the time by watching the other passengers, trying to distract herself from her nerves. They seem so at ease, so accustomed to leaving and returning, to making lives for themselves beyond the familiar boundaries of home.

Erin shifts uncomfortably in her seat, her head full of the stories she'd been told about city life—stories that made Dublin seem like a bustling, chaotic place.

The people there move quickly and didn't stop to talk, didn't nod or say hello like they do in Tyrone. She wonders if she'll even fit in if her accent and small-town manners will make her stick out like a sore thumb.

By the time they cross the border, her nerves have grown into a dull throb of anxiety. Every fibre of her is screaming to turn back.

She can practically hear her friends in Tyrone saying, "It is a wild idea, anyway, thinking you could handle Dublin."

But then the bus pulls into the city, and the streets and buildings rise up around her like walls. Dublin is bigger, louder and more intense than she'd imagined. The streets teeming with people, cars honking, buses rumbling past, and everyone moving with purpose. She clutches her bag, feeling small and conspicuous.

When Erin steps off the bus in Dublin, the city feels even more intimidating than she had anticipated. She gathers her things and looks around, trying to find some sense of familiarity in the bustling streets.

But there is nothing—just streams of strangers moving in every direction, none of them noticing her, a girl from the countryside in Tyrone, slightly lost in their midst. Again, she wraps her arms tightly around her bag for comfort, suddenly aware of how far from home she is, and feels the pang of homesickness intensify.

Without looking back, she starts off towards the address of her new digs, clutching the slip of paper she'd scrawled it on as if it were a lifeline.

Her accommodation, as it turns out, is a box room in a shared apartment in the heart of the city. When she pushes open the door, she is met with a narrow bed wedged against the wall, a single wardrobe with a missing handle, and a small window that lets in just a sliver of light.

She drops her bags and takes it all in, feeling both the thrill of independence and the bite of reality. This is her new life—a far cry from the open fields and wide skies of Tyrone, but it is hers nonetheless.

The first night, though, as she lies on the hard mattress listening to the sounds of the city filter through the thin walls, she wonders if she has made the right decision to come here.

The next morning, she rises early, her nerves tangling as she prepares for her first shift at Eddie Rocket's. The little diner, known for its retro style and fast-paced atmosphere, is a popular spot in the city, and she landed the job just before moving down.

Walking through its glass doors, she feels a jolt of excitement mixed with apprehension. She knows she'll be on her feet all day, and the diner's buzz is already in full swing when she arrives.

"New girl?" comes a voice from behind the counter.

She turns to see a tall, dark-haired man grinning at her with an easy, open expression. He is already in his uniform—black shirt, red apron, and a nametag that reads Fabio. He seems comfortable here, leaning back against the counter like he belonged.

"Yes," she replied, feeling slightly awkward under his gaze. "I'm Erin."

His smile widened, as if he found her accent charming, though he couldn't hide a slight look of puzzlement.

"I'm from Tyrone," Erin said after recognising his bewilderment.

"Ah, Tyrone," he said slowly as if he were tasting the unfamiliar name on his tongue. "I don't think I've met anyone from there."

"Well, Erin from Tyrone, welcome to the madness," he said with a laugh, his accent unmistakably Brazilian, warm and musical. "They've got me on the grill today, but I'm happy to show you the ropes whenever you're ready."

He tilted his head with a grin. "I've been here a while—I know all the best tricks for sneaking in a break."

Erin laughs, a bit more at ease, and nods at him gratefully. Fabio has an effortless charm that somehow softens the unfamiliarity of her surroundings. He is striking, with tanned skin and dark eyes that seem to gleam with a quiet confidence.

Fabio had been working at Eddie Rocket's for over two years, she soon learns, and he knows the place like the back of his hand. Erin watches as he handles orders with easy precision, flipping burgers and cracking jokes with the other staff, making everyone feel just a bit more at ease.

As the day wore on, Erin finds herself gravitating towards him. He was patient, showing her everything from where to find the condiments to how to manage the rush-hour crowd.

His instructions are always punctuated by a friendly smile or a joke that makes her laugh. By the end of her shift, she feels like she has found an unexpected friend in the chaos of Dublin.

Over the next few days, Erin and Fabio's friendship deepens. Working side by side in the heat and bustle of Eddie Rocket's, they share stories of their hometowns and laugh over the quirks of city life.

Fabio teaches her the unspoken rules of Dublin—the way people don't greet each other in passing, the importance of moving quickly, of blending in. It is strange for Erin, who is used to smiling at everyone she passed back in Tyrone, but Fabio's advice helps her adjust to her new life.

Outside of work, they sometimes grab a coffee or take a walk through the city together, and Erin finds herself looking forward to these moments more than she wants to admit.

He has a knack for making her feel like she belongs here; like she is capable of handling whatever this big, intimidating city throws her way.

Slowly, Erin realises that her life is no longer just about surviving in Dublin. Fabio's warmth and humour make her feel alive in ways she hadn't expected; drawing her out of her shell and helping her grow comfortable in her own skin.

What started as a simple job and an act of courage in leaving Tyrone is turning into something far more than Erin could have imagined.

Days turn into weeks, and Erin finds herself spending more and more time with Fabio. He is a patient guide, showing her everything from the best cafes to the quiet corners of St Stephen's Green, where the hum of the city fades into birdsong and the rustle of leaves.

He introduces her to new foods and even got her to try salsa dancing one night, though she is hopelessly clumsy. Fabio laughed the whole time, his hands firm and steady as they guide her through each misstep.

There is a steadiness to him, a feeling of ease that puts her at peace. She admires his confidence, the way he navigates Dublin with a grace she envies.

When she confessed how overwhelmed she still felt at times, he simply shrugged, saying, "You're stronger than you think, Erin. It's just a city—it can't beat you."

Over time, she finds herself letting go of her homesickness, growing accustomed to the rush of people and the loud honking of cars, and even finding comfort in the anonymity of it all. She is surprised by how much she has changed, but she knows it isn't just Dublin—it is Fabio.

Their friendship blossoms into something deeper, almost without her realising it. Late nights spent laughing at small cafes, lazy afternoons strolling by the river, stolen glances that linger just a moment too long—it all blurs into a beautiful haze.

Fabio seems to see something in her, something Erin hadn't known she was hiding. He makes her feel like she can be anyone and do anything.

One evening, as they walk along the River Liffey, Erin turns to Fabio, her heart hammering.

"Thank you," she said, her voice barely above a whisper.

"For what?"

"For…everything. For showing me this world, for making me feel like I belong here."

Fabio looks back at her, his expression softening. He reaches out, brushing a strand of hair away from her face.

"You do belong here, Erin. You're not the same girl who stepped off that bus. Dublin suits you. And—" he hesitates, his gaze dropping before he continues, "I think I'd miss you if you went back."

With that, he leans over, pulls her in towards him, and they share their first kiss.

As they stand there, the city lights reflecting in the water, Erin feels her heart swell with a new sense of belonging. She realises, with a sudden clarity, that Fabio isn't just her guide to Dublin—he has become her home here; the person she wants to build a life around.

Over the next months, their love grows, their lives intertwining in ways Erin didn't anticipate. Fabio taught her to embrace the city's fast pace, to find beauty in its quirks and eccentricities. And Erin, with her quiet resilience and fierce loyalty, gave Fabio something he has been missing: a sense of steadiness and belonging.

For a while, they are inseparable, wrapped up in their own world, and Erin feels she has found her place at last. She has left Tyrone with a heart full of fear, but now, thanks to Fabio, she is learning to live without it.

Chapter Two

In the early days of Erin and Fabio's relationship, it's as though every moment they share sparkles with possibility. Erin feels like she is in a dream she doesn't want to wake up from; she has never felt this way about anyone before.

She is wrapped up in a whirlwind of passion and happiness that seems almost too perfect to be real.

Dublin, once so intimidating and unfamiliar, begins to feel like home because of Fabio. He is her anchor in the bustling city, guiding her through its fast-paced life with ease and charm.

Together, they explore the streets hand in hand; laughing as they dodge traffic; stopping to listen to street musicians and sharing late-night coffees at cafes tucked into quiet alleyways. It is in those small, stolen moments that Erin finds herself falling harder each day.

Fabio has a way of making even the simplest things feel magical. He leads her to places she's never been before, charming her with stories and little discoveries. He helps her to live in the present, to enjoy every second without worrying about what will come next.

His laughter is contagious, and Erin feels her own world opening up in ways she hasn't expected. She can feel herself changing, becoming braver, more confident, and more willing to take risks.

Their time together is filled with easy, joyful moments, like walking along the River Liffey or sharing a pint at a local pub. Also, the thrilling ones like sneaking into a fancy rooftop party or dancing together on the street after midnight.

When they are together, everything feels right, even perfect. Erin finds herself opening up in ways she'd never dared with anyone else, sharing her fears, her dreams and her hopes, and he listens, making her feel valued and cherished.

Erin loves how Fabio looks at her like she is the most important person in the world. The way he holds her hand or tucks a stray strand of hair behind her ear makes her feel safe and adored.

He speaks to her with such warmth, like she is his muse. His poetic phrases make her feel like she is living in one of the old romantic films they sometimes watch together.

Their connection is electric, intense yet comforting, and Erin can't imagine her life without him. She'd catch herself smiling just thinking about him, anticipating the next time they'd be together.

She'd never known love could feel like this—a mix of exhilaration, tenderness, and a deep sense of belonging.

They would spend late nights talking about their future, their dreams for life beyond Dublin, and the things they wanted to experience together. Fabio would sometimes talk about his family back in Brazil, and Erin could see a deep love for them in his eyes. She dreams of meeting them someday, of travelling the world together, hand in hand.

As Erin looks at Fabio, she can't help but think that she has found the person she is meant to be with. She is head over heels, for the kind of love that feels like the foundation for everything else in her life. And in these moments, she imagines they will be together forever.

But as the months pass, she begins to notice subtle changes, like a chill creeping into a warm room. At first, it is easy to brush off his comments and behaviours as harmless quirks or maybe his own insecurities. If he questions her about her plans or asks who she is spending time with, she figures he is just protective.

"It's nice to have someone care about me this much," she tells herself.

But with time, his protectiveness becomes something else.

The first real sign comes during a casual night out with friends from work. They all go out for drinks after a busy shift, and Fabio, despite his usual charm, has been oddly quiet, sticking close to her side, his hand is wrapped a bit too tightly around her waist.

Erin catches him watching her as she laughs and chats with their friends. He looks tense, his jaw set in a way that doesn't fit the carefree Fabio she has known. Later, as they leave, he asks her why she'd laughed so much at one of their male coworker's jokes.

"Oh, he's just funny, you know?" she replies with a small shrug, not thinking anything of it.

But Fabio remained quiet for the rest of the walk home, and she could feel his mood darken, lingering like a shadow between them.

Over the next few months, his behaviour continues to shift. Little by little, Fabio seems to need her in ways that leave her feeling trapped instead of cherished. He begins calling her constantly when they are apart, asking where she is and who she is with.

If she didn't pick up immediately, he'd leave a string of messages, each one more insistent than the last. When she finally answers, he'd be angry, accusing her of ignoring him, of putting other people before him.

"Don't you care about me?" he would say, his voice wounded, and she finds herself apologising, promising to be more attentive.

His words would cut into her, and she'd wonder if maybe she was doing something wrong. Each time she tries to pull back a bit—to make space for her own friends or hobbies—he would find ways to pull her back in; to make her feel guilty for wanting time away from him.

Erin begins to notice how easily, and more frequently, his mood can shift. One moment, he'll be joking and smiling, and the next, he'll turn dark and quiet, looking at her with an intensity that feels almost like resentment.

His grip on her arm tightened, his voice low and cold as he asked, "What were you talking to that guy about? Or why were you smiling at him like that?"

Each time, she'd try to reassure him, brushing off his suspicions with a laugh or a quick kiss, hoping he'd understand that she was his, that she loved him. But nothing seems to quiet his fears.

The city, Erin had once felt thrilling and full of possibility, starts to feel small and oppressive. Fabio has opinions on every aspect of her life—what she wears, who she spends time with, and even how she does her hair. He will comment on her appearance before they go out, sometimes with a slight sneer.

"You're really going to wear that?" he'll say, his eyes scanning her with a look that makes her feel self-conscious.

Slowly, almost without realising it, she begins to dress the way he prefers, keeping her makeup minimal, and her clothes more conservative.

When she meets up with her coworkers or her few new friends, Fabio always needs to know where she is going and who will be there. This can't go on she thought to herself.

Then, one day, Erin sat on the edge of their bed, staring out the window as the sky shifts into an overcast grey, mirroring the heaviness in her heart. Her life in Dublin has turned into something she no longer recognises.

The vibrant, joyful relationship she once shared with Fabio now feels like a series of heavy chains binding her to him. Each time she thought about leaving, a wave of guilt and confusion would wash over her. She doesn't recognise herself in this state of constant indecision, and it scares her.

Over the past few months, she has carefully tucked away every little sign and red flag in hopes that Fabio's behaviour will change. Maybe he was just going through a rough patch, she'd reasoned, feeling trapped in his possessiveness but unsure if walking away was the answer.

Some part of her still holds onto the version of him she'd fallen in love with—the man who'd shown her Dublin; taught her everything she knew about the city and made her laugh like no one else had. But lately, it's as if that man has vanished, leaving her alone with someone she can hardly recognise.

At times, she tells herself that she just needs to be patient; that maybe he'll return to his old self if she can be a little more understanding, a little more loving.

But as she wrestles with the idea of leaving, she feels a new sense of relief begin to form in her mind, as if the weight on her chest might finally lift if she could only find the courage to let him go. She knows it will be hard, painful even, but she can't shake the feeling that it might be the only way for her to truly feel like herself again.

One night, as they sit across the dinner table from each other in tense silence, Erin's gaze keeps dropping to her plate, and her mind churns through all the possibilities. Fabio's eyes flicker over to her, and she can tell he senses her distance. Suddenly, he broke the silence, reaching across the table to take her hand, his fingers firm around hers.

"Erin," he said, his voice unusually soft, almost vulnerable. "I know things haven't been…easy between us lately. I know I've been difficult." He hesitates, his eyes searching hers. "I just…I've been feeling lost. Being away from home, my friends, my family—it's been harder than I thought it would be."

Erin feels her defences falter. She never expected this from him, this raw honesty that she hadn't seen in so long. His eyes looked so sincere, his voice almost pleading, as if he were baring a part of himself, he'd kept hidden.

She feels a small pang of empathy, remembering her own feelings of loneliness when she'd first arrived in Dublin. Maybe he is struggling in ways she hasn't understood.

"Why didn't you tell me?" she asks, her voice barely a whisper.

"I didn't want to burden you," he said, running a hand through his hair. "But I've been feeling…trapped here, cut off from everything I know. And then, there you are, making friends, adjusting to everything so well, while I'm—"

He trails off, his eyes clouded with a mixture of frustration and sadness. "I guess I just started taking it out on you without even realising it."

His admission hung in the air, and for a moment, Erin felt her anger and frustration soften. She can see the truth in his words—she can feel his pain. It is a side of him she hasn't seen before, and it tugs at her heart, reigniting a glimmer of hope that maybe they can still work things out.

"I know I've been too much sometimes," he continues, his grip on her hand tightening. "But I don't want to lose you, Erin. I need you. I love you."

Erin's breath caught as he spoke those words, and a small part of her heart ached, remembering why she'd fallen in love with him in the first place.

She still cares deeply for him, despite everything. She wants to believe that they can make this work, that he can change, that they can find their way back to the laughter and warmth they'd once shared.

He leans forward, his voice low and intense. "Come with me to Brazil. Let me show you my world, my home, my family. Maybe…maybe that will help me feel like myself again. I swear, if you come with me, I'll change. Things will be different."

She hesitates again, weighing his words, feeling the pull of his sincerity but also the whisper of doubt lingering in the back of her mind. She wants to believe him. She wants so desperately to think that this trip could be a fresh start, a way to salvage what was left of their love.

But she also couldn't ignore the nagging feeling that this was her last shot—that if things didn't improve after this, she'll have to walk away.

"But...you've promised me before that things would change," she said quietly, pulling her hand back and searching his face. "How can I know that this time will be different?"

He takes a deep breath, his shoulders slumping slightly. "Because this time, I'm not just saying it, Erin. I'm showing you. I'm bringing you into my life, into everything that matters to me. I know I've been selfish. I know I've hurt you. But I'm asking you to give me one more chance. Just one more."

Erin bites her lip, her mind racing. She thinks about the person she used to be, the girl who moved to Dublin with dreams in her heart, a sense of adventure, and a spirit that felt free and light. She misses that girl. She misses feeling like herself.

But looking into Fabio's eyes, she sees a glimpse of the man she'd fallen in love with, the one who'd made her believe in herself and pushed her to embrace the world around her. Maybe, just maybe, that man was still there, buried beneath the jealousy and possessiveness that had clouded their relationship.

"Okay," she said finally, her voice steady but tentative. "I'll go with you. But this...this is it, Fabio. If things don't change if I feel like this again—" She trails off, unable to finish the sentence, but the meaning hangs heavily between them.

He nods solemnly, a flicker of relief flashing in his eyes. "I promise, Erin. I'll make things right. I'll show you that I can be the man you fell in love with."

With a deep breath, Erin forces herself to believe him, to hope that maybe this trip will bring them closer again and heal the rifts that have widened between them.

She still loves him, even with all the doubts and fears, and she knows that if there is a chance to save their relationship, she has to take it. This was their last chance, and she clung to it with everything she had.

As the days pass, Erin feels a cautious excitement start to build alongside her doubts. She finds herself imagining what it will be like to meet his family, to see the places he has spoken of with such warmth and nostalgia.

Perhaps, she thought, being in his home country can help him soften, help him find the peace he seems to be searching for. She wants so badly for this trip to be their fresh start, to bring them back to the way they once had been.

On the day of their departure, as they board the plane to Brazil, Erin casts one last glance at Dublin from the airport window. A flicker of hope rose in her chest, mixed with the apprehension that won't quite fade.

She clings to the idea that this is the beginning of a new chapter, that maybe Fabio is right, and he just needs to reconnect with his roots.

With a deep breath, she takes her seat next to him, feeling his hand close around hers, strong and reassuring. She squeezes his hand, allowing herself to believe that perhaps things can change, that maybe their love will withstand this final test.

The future feels uncertain, but as she looks into his eyes, she holds on to the hope that this journey will bring them closer; that she will finally find the love she once had when she'd first arrived in Dublin.

But as the plane lifts off, Erin still can't shake the small, nagging voice deep inside her, the one that warns her to be careful, to guard her heart. Because if this trip doesn't change things, she knows she'll have no choice but to find the courage to leave Fabio. And that thought, as painful as it was, gave her the strength to hold on and give it one last try.

Chapter Three

The warmth of Brazil embraces Erin as soon as she steps off the plane. Sunlight dances off the palm trees, the air rich with scents of unfamiliar flowers and a gentle, salty breeze from the ocean. As they drive through Fabio's hometown, she marvels at the colourful streets and vibrant energy all around her.

Everywhere she looks, there is something new and beautiful—old colonial buildings painted in bright hues. Busy markets are filled with people laughing and bartering, and a cacophony of Portuguese that makes her smile, even if she can't understand it.

Fabio had changed almost instantly upon their arrival. His eyes are alight with excitement and warmth, a side of him she hasn't seen in an age. Here, he seems to come alive, his gestures are more relaxed, his laugh comes easier, and his smile is broader.

He introduced her to everyone with pride, his hand firm around hers as he led her through the town and into the embrace of his family and friends.

His mother hugs Erin as though they have known each other for years, her face lighting up as she chats warmly in

Portuguese. Even though Erin can't understand every word, the love and acceptance are unmistakable.

Fabio's father claps her on the back, welcoming her with a huge grin, and his friends greet her with a mixture of curiosity and enthusiasm. The kindness and laughter around her remind her of home, and it feels good—better than she'd expected.

In these first few days, Erin's heart softens as she watches Fabio blend effortlessly into his surroundings. She sees the man she had first fallen for, the one who taught her how to navigate the bustling streets of Dublin.

The one who introduced her to city life with laughter and confidence. Now, seeing him in his own element, she feels that familiar warmth return, the spark that had first drawn her to him.

They spend the days exploring his old town, wandering through markets, and visiting local spots where he'd grown up. He shows her the beach he'd frequented as a child, the hill where he and his friends would watch the sunset and the small, lively cafes where they'd spent their teenage years.

Watching Fabio here, Erin realises just how deeply she loves him. This side of him, the carefree, happy man she sees now, is worth fighting for. She allows herself to imagine a future together. To picture what it will be like to build a life here, in this place where he feels so alive.

On their fourth night, Fabio suggests they go out with his childhood friends. Erin feels a flutter of excitement; she wants to connect with his friends, to understand more about the people who'd shaped him. They meet up at a lively club in town, the music is loud, the crowd laughing and dancing; a vibrant atmosphere that makes Erin feel both energised and a bit nervous.

She makes an extra effort to be friendly, smiling and chatting with Fabio's friends, trying to bridge the language gap with laughter and warm gestures. She wants them to like her, to feel like she belongs.

She dances with Fabio, then with one of his female friends who pulls her onto the dance floor, and she laughs as they spin and twirl to the beat. She feels a rush of joy, revelling in the feeling of connection and freedom.

But as the night goes on, she notices Fabio watching her with a dark intensity. His face, which had been open and happy, is now closed off. His eyes are following her every move, but his expression is unreadable.

She tries to ignore it, hoping he is just tired, that maybe he is just getting used to seeing her in this new social setting.

As the music pounds and the lights flicker, Fabio approaches her, his jaw clenched. He grabs her arm, pulling her aside with a force that takes her breath away.

"What do you think you're doing?" he hissed, his face inches from hers, his grip like a vice on her arm.

"W-What do you mean?" she stammers, taken aback. "I'm just trying to get to know your friends. I thought you'd be happy—"

"Happy?" His voice dripped with contempt. "You think I'm happy watching you flirt with my friends? Laughing, dancing like that? You think I don't see what you're doing?"

"Flirting? Fabio, I was just being friendly," she said, her voice trembling, trying to keep her composure.

But he didn't listen.

His face twisted with anger as he leans closer. "I'm not stupid, Erin. You were all over them, trying to make a fool out of me."

Before she could say another word, he grabbed her wrist, dragging her through the crowded club and out into the night air. She struggles against his grip, panic rising as she feels her feet stumble along the rough pavement. Outside, he releases her only to grip her by the hair, his face inches from hers.

"Let go of me, Fabio!" she gasps, fear and disbelief surging through her.

But he only tightens his hold, his eyes flashing with anger. Erin's heart pounds as she realises that the man she'd fallen in love with has vanished again; leaving her with someone she barely recognises. The bliss of the past few days feels like a distant memory, washed away by the fury in his eyes.

Desperate and terrified, Erin yanks herself free, her heart racing as she darts towards his family's cruiser parked nearby. She jumps into the driver's seat, her hands shaking as she fumbles for the keys. Her mind reeling with the need to get away. To escape before he could do anything else.

As she starts the engine, she sees Fabio advancing towards the car, his face twisted with rage. She throws the car into gear, her hands clench the wheel, her vision blurring as tears threaten to spill over. In her panic, she doesn't notice him standing so close until she feels a jolt—a sickening thud as the car's side mirror clips him.

She sees him crumple to the pavement, his head hitting the ground with a dull smack, his body motionless under the glow of the streetlights.

Erin's heart seizes in her chest as she stares at his still form, her breath catching in horror. She only wants to escape, to protect herself. Now, as she sits there, hands trembling on the wheel, a surge of guilt and fear washes over her.

The reality of what has happened, settles heavily in her mind, mingling with the terror that had driven her to this moment.

For a second, she considers getting out of the car, rushing to his side, checking if he was okay. But as she glances around the empty street, the fear returns, sharper than ever. She knows that staying here could mean facing his wrath all over again, and that thought terrifies her more than anything.

With a shaky breath, she presses her foot down on the accelerator, speeding away into the night. Her mind is a blur of panic, guilt, and the sobering realisation that her life has just irrevocably changed. With this thought, Erin loses herself in a traumatic trance and has no recollection of how she got to where she is now.

In the harsh, blinding lights of a hospital hallway, Erin sits in a hard, plastic chair, her hands trembling, her heart racing, her mind spinning with shock and dread.

Hours had passed since she'd left Fabio lying on the pavement. She had somehow been found, questioned, and brought to this hospital where he was now in a medically induced coma.

She still hasn't fully absorbed what has happened, her mind stuck in a cycle of disbelief and horror. What started as an attempt to escape from a violent outburst has unravelled into something unfathomable.

After the incident, Erin had driven aimlessly, her mind reeling, hands gripped tight on the steering wheel as she tried to make sense of what she had done. Her plan, if she had even had one, was just to get away—to find a safe place to think, to breathe.

She barely understands where she is when police lights flash behind her, illuminating the dark road. It hadn't taken long for them to surround her, guns drawn, their voices loud and unyielding as they ordered her out of the car.

Now, she sits in a stark room, with an officer questioning her, her thoughts clouded by panic and confusion. She tries to explain, her voice cracking as she tells them what had happened; how Fabio dragged her out of the club in a fit of rage, how she'd only wanted to escape to protect herself.

But her words seem to fall on deaf ears. The officers look at each other, unconvinced, their faces set in grim lines. To them, she was a foreigner who had committed an unforgivable act on their soil. She can feel the weight of their distrust as she tries to make them understand.

There were no witnesses to see how Fabio grabbed her, no one who has seen the panic that had driven her to flee. All they had were a few witnesses outside the club who had seen her speed off in the family's car, striking Fabio as he approached. And that was all they needed. In their eyes, she tried to kill him.

The next day, they charge her formally. She is to be held in prison, pending trial and sentencing. The weight of those words presses down on her, but it isn't until she arrives at the facility that the full reality of her situation strikes her.

She is escorted through tall iron gates into a high-security prison known to house some of Brazil's most dangerous offenders. The guards say little as they lead her down dimly lit hallways, past cells with barred windows and eyes staring at her from every direction. She feels exposed, vulnerable and completely isolated in a country that was supposed to have been her escape.

Her cell is stark and cold, with a narrow cot, a metal toilet, and a thin window high on the wall that lets in just a sliver of sunlight during the day. The walls bear the marks of previous inhabitants—scratches, etched symbols, angry words in Portuguese. Everything feels foreign, alien and unyielding like she has been cast into a different world.

Days turn into weeks as Erin struggles to adapt to the brutal reality of prison life. She is surrounded by women whose lives have hardened them, women who stare at her with distrust, suspicion, and sometimes outright hostility.

She keeps to herself, afraid to speak, her broken Portuguese barely enough to communicate. Every sound seems magnified here—the clang of metal doors, the muttered conversations, the harsh commands of the guards.

The atmosphere is thick with tension and violence. Fights break out regularly, and she learns quickly to keep her head down, to avoid drawing attention. She spends most of her days in silence, replaying the night of the incident over and over in her mind, trying to find a different outcome, another way it could have gone that wouldn't have led her here.

She thinks about Fabio lying in the hospital, his fate uncertain. The thought that she might have hurt him so gravely fills her with guilt and confusion. She loved him, despite the pain he had caused her, despite the moments of fear. Now, even though she'd been driven by self-preservation, she feels as though she has betrayed everything, she once believed in.

The guards have little patience for her, viewing her as yet another foreigner who has come to their country and created trouble. They are cold, dismissive, and quick to show her that she has no special treatment here. Erin quickly learns that compassion is scarce, and trust is something she can't afford to give.

Every day is a battle to protect herself, to remain as invisible as possible; hoping to avoid the attention of other inmates who seem to sense her vulnerability.

In the rare moments when she allows herself to feel hope, Erin imagines her trial, clinging to the faint idea that her story might eventually be believed.

But each passing day erodes that hope a little more, as she watches other women being dragged into courtrooms only to return with sentences that seem unending. She fears that her side of the story will never be heard. Her words will mean little against the cold, hard facts of what had happened.

Some days, she feels an overwhelming sense of despair, a deep and hollow ache that settles in her chest as she thinks about her family and her hometown in Tyrone. She wonders what they have heard, what they must think of her now.

She left Ireland with the hope of rekindling her love for Fabio, only to find herself in a prison, thousands of miles away, fighting for her life and her freedom. The dream she'd once held of a future with Fabio seems like a distant illusion. Like a memory of someone she used to be, someone, who believed in love and happiness.

One evening, a guard comes to her cell with a brief update: Fabio is still in a coma, and his condition is critical. Erin nods, her throat tight, swallowing back the emotions that surge inside her.

Part of her still wished for him to wake up, if only to prove that she has not truly taken everything from him. But she also fears what his awakening will mean, what he will say, and what accusations might await her. She knows that without his account, her chances at trial were bleak.

Without witnesses to back her up, she was at the mercy of a system she barely understood, in a place that is seemingly determined to break her.

Alone in her cell, Erin often lies awake, her mind drifting between memories and fears. The love she'd felt for Fabio clashed with the anger and betrayal that simmers within her, creating a constant, restless ache.

She tried so hard to make their relationship work, to see the good in him, to believe in a future where they could find happiness. Now, that hope is shattered, replaced by the brutal reality of her confinement. The love she had fought for so fiercely, seems to have led her only into darkness.

Weeks turn into months, and the prospect of sentencing looms on the horizon like a shadow. Erin faces it with a hollow resignation, knowing that no amount of explaining and no desperate pleas, would change what she had done—or how it looked to the people around her.

Her fate seems sealed in the eyes of the court, and as she lies in the cold darkness of her cell each night, she can feel the weight of her actions pressing down on her, leaving her with nothing but the quiet, inescapable truth.

Chapter Four

Each meeting that Erin has with the assigned lawyer is becoming less and less comforting. The first time she was introduced to Carlos was on her fourth day incarcerated. She was taken from her cell and escorted to a dingy room with a table in the middle.

On the other side of the desk was a man in an ill-fitting stained suit. There was a pungent smell of stale sweat, and his breath stank of coffee and cigarettes. His hair was greasy and unwashed, just like the rest of him.

He barely looked up when Erin was led into the room. Instead, he gestured for her to sit as he shuffled through a stack of papers.

"Miss O'Connell, your case is…well, it's complicated, to say the least," he began, his voice heavy with disinterest.

"My name is O'Connor by the way, and I don't think it's that complicated."

Carlos finally raised his head and looked at her, expression blank.

"We'll aim for leniency, of course," he had said, as though it were some throwaway remarks.

Leniency? Erin wanted to scream.

She didn't want leniency. She wants freedom. She wants someone to fight for her, not scrape together a half-hearted plea deal. She left that first meeting in a daze of shock and disgust. This man wasn't going to fight for her. She had to get him replaced, but for that to happen, then she would need help.

Erin remembers her first phone call to her mother, remembers every phone call to her mother, actually. At first, Erin's mother's voice on the other end of the scratchy prison phone line is a lifeline; a fragment of home that keeps her tethered to sanity. In those initial days, Mrs O'Connor had been frantic, her concern almost suffocating.

"Oh, Erin, what in God's name is going on? I can barely think straight since we heard. Are they treating you alright in there? Jesus, you must be so frightened. Your father's been up all night pacing the floor. We're worried sick," she said, her words tumbling over one another in a breathless stream.

Erin clings to the phone, tears slipping down her cheeks as she imagines her family sitting in the cramped kitchen of their little house in Tyrone, just as she'd left them all those years ago.

The thought of her father pacing, her mother fretting over the kettle, her extended family quietly listening from the next room—it was almost enough to comfort her.

"Please, Ma. I need your help," Erin whispered, her throat tight. "Can you find me a better lawyer? This fella doesn't care if I rot in here. He's useless. Please, Ma, I can't do this on my own."

Her mother hesitated. "We'll see what we can do, love. We'll ask around, alright? Don't worry yourself. Just…keep your chin up."

Initially, Erin didn't detect the hesitance in her mother's voice. She went back to her cell that night filled with hope, and almost expectance that her mother will make everything go away. As the days passed along, and the phone calls offered no resolution to her lawyer problem, Erin's realisation begins to hit home.

"Please, Ma," Erin whispered again, her voice hoarse from days of pleading. "I do really need help. This lawyer is useless. Can you not find someone else? Someone decent?"

There was a long pause on the other end, followed by another vague and hesitant response. "We're...looking into it, love. We'll see what we can do."

Her stomach churns. The words offered no comfort, no commitment, only an evasive promise that left her feeling more alone than ever. She bit down on her lip to keep from crying, the salty sting of desperation sharp on her tongue.

"I'm begging you, Ma. Please. He doesn't care if I go down for this or not. I can't do this by myself."

"I know, pet," her mother said softly, but there was no urgency in her voice, no fire that Erin needed so badly to hear. "We'll talk again soon, alright?"

Before Erin could press further, the line is dead. She stares at the receiver for a moment before placing it back on its cradle, her hands trembling.

And as the days continue to drag into weeks, the tone of those calls began to shift. The urgency in her mother's voice softened, replaced by something harder to define—exasperation? Distance? It gnawed at Erin, who felt increasingly adrift, her pleas for help falling into a widening chasm.

By the third or fourth call, Erin notices that her mother no longer asks about her day or her condition. Instead, the conversations had become punctuated by long silences and deflections.

"Have you heard anything yet about the trial date?" Erin asked one evening, gripping the receiver tightly.

The pay phone in the prison's common room was sticky with grime, and the murmurs of other inmates around her makes it hard to concentrate.

"Not yet, love," her mother replied distractedly. "But listen, we've had the neighbours calling around...asking questions. You know what people are like."

Erin blinked, confused. "What kind of questions?"

"Oh, you know. Nosy ones. About what happened, about Fabio. Some of them even had the cheek to say you were always too wild, running off to Dublin and all." Her mother's voice dropped, and Erin could hear the edge of bitterness there, sharp and unexpected.

"It's putting awful strain on your father. His heart, Erin...it's not good. He has been so worked up about it."

Erin's stomach twisted. "I didn't mean for this to happen, Ma. You know that, right?"

"I know, love. But you've no idea how hard it is for us here. Your father has been to the doctor twice this week. And people keep staring at me in the shop like I've done something wrong. It's not easy."

"It's not easy?" Erin's voice rose, a rare flash of anger breaking through her usual defeat. "I'm in here, Ma! In this place, where no one cares if you live or die. And you're worried about what the neighbours think?"

Her mother didn't respond for a moment.

When she finally spoke, her tone was clipped. "Don't you raise your voice at me, Erin O'Connor. I've enough on my plate without you adding to it. We're doing our best, alright?"

The call ended soon after, leaving Erin staring at the scratched receiver as if it had betrayed her.

Each subsequent call only deepened the rift. Her mother's words, once full of warmth and worry, now seem cold, short, and occasionally barbed.

"Have you spoken to the lawyer?" Erin asked desperately during one call, her hands trembling as she held the phone.

"I did," her mother replied, her voice brisk. "He said he's doing everything he can. He's the one who knows the law, Erin, not us."

"But he's not doing enough! He doesn't even listen to me—"

"Maybe if you hadn't gotten yourself into this mess, we wouldn't be having this conversation," her mother snapped suddenly, then immediately sighed. "Sorry. That was unfair. But you don't know what it's like here, Erin. And your father…well, he's not been himself at all. He's had to take time off work because people wouldn't stop asking him questions."

Erin's heart sinks. Every call seems to follow the same pattern: her mother's initial show of concern quickly giving way to updates about the village gossip, the strain on her father, and the toll it was taking on the family.

By the sixth or seventh call, Erin feels like she is speaking to a stranger.

"You don't sound well, Ma," Erin said one evening, trying to keep the frustration out of her voice.

"Well, how do you expect me to sound? I'm doing everything I can to hold this family together," her mother shot back. "Do you know how hard it is for your father to even look at the neighbours anymore? People are saying terrible things, Erin. And your poor father—"

"What about me?" Erin interrupted, her voice breaking. "Does anyone care about what's happening to me? About what I'm going through?"

"Of course, we care," her mother replied sharply. "But you have to understand, Erin. This isn't just happening to you. It's happening to all of us."

After that, Erin stopped asking her family for help. She has stopped begging her mother to find her a better lawyer or asking if anyone would come to the trial.

She simply calls out of habit, listening quietly as her mother speaks about everything except Erin's situation: the price of petrol, the weather in Tyrone, and the new curtains she is planning to buy for the living room.

It is a relief, in some ways, when the call time ran out. Erin hangs up the receiver and returns to her cell, feeling hollow and more alone than ever.

Her family has not explicitly abandoned her, not in the way that some inmates' families did. But they have distanced themselves just enough to let Erin feel the sting of it. It wasn't the silence that hurt—it was the casual indifference masquerading as concern.

The cell block is silent except for the occasional shuffle of heavy boots against the concrete floor. Erin O'Connor sits hunched on her thin mattress, clutching the battered receiver of the wall-mounted phone. The line crackles an unwelcome reminder of the distance between her and home.

The days before the trial are an agonising blur. Each hour feels like a slow crawl through molasses, yet at the same time, they race by too quickly, leaving Erin breathless and unprepared.

Her cell becomes a vortex of uncertainty and tension. The walls seem to close in tighter with each passing day, the once-tolerable smells of damp concrete and stale air were now nauseating her.

Sleep is a distant memory, which is replaced by endless hours of staring at the cracked ceiling, her mind looping through the same relentless questions:

Will they come? Will I have to face this alone?

Erin clung to the phone calls, despite their diminishing returns. She sits on the cold bench by the payphone, the receiver pressing to her ear, waiting for her mother's voice to ground her.

"Well, we're thinking about it," her mother said the last time Erin asked if they'd come to Brazil for the trial. "It's a lot, Erin. You know how your father is, and there's so much to do here—"

So much to do here.

Erin has no response to that. What is there to do in Tyrone that could outweigh showing up for your daughter?

After the calls, Erin retreats to her cell, consumed by a whirlwind of hope and despair. Sometimes, her mind betrays her with visions of them surprising her on the first day of the trial; walking into the courtroom and taking their place in the gallery. Her mother, dabbing her eyes with a tissue, her father sitting stiff-backed but present.

It is a comforting thought, and it makes Erin's heart swell for a brief, foolish moment. But that hope always came crashing down, leaving her feeling hollower than before. Deep down, she knows better. Her family don't want to face the gossip or the judgment from their neighbours. They are ashamed of her.

Erin finds herself obsessing over every detail in the prison; watching for signs and patterns, as though reading the environment can give her some clue about what was to come.

Her lawyer, Mr Greasy Hair, has stopped visiting as regularly, leaving Erin feeling more abandoned than ever, which she didn't think was possible. His few appearances were hardly reassuring. He shuffles into the visitation room with his tattered briefcase, barely making eye contact as he rattles off procedural updates in a monotone voice.

"Can you at least tell me if my family will be allowed to testify?" she asked, gripping the edge of the table.

The lawyer blinked as if she'd asked him to recite advanced calculus. "Well, if they show up, I suppose they could."

If they show up.

The words hang in the air like a death knell.

There were moments when Erin couldn't help but let hope take over, no matter how fleeting. Sometimes, in the quiet hours of the night, she pictures her mother standing in the kitchen back home, her fingers busy with some mindless task—peeling potatoes, kneading dough—but her thoughts were entirely on Erin.

Maybe, just maybe, she can convince herself that they can't bear the thought of her alone in that courtroom. Maybe they are packing their bags at that very moment, preparing to drive to Dublin.

Those thoughts carry her through the night, bringing a faint smile to her lips. But by morning, the cold light of reality sweeps the illusions away. She wakes up in her cell, the distant clang of metal doors reminding her that she was alone and that her hope had been nothing more than a cruel trick of her mind.

The next day, she finds herself sitting in the cramped visitor's room, the smell of disinfectant and damp metal permeating the air. Her lawyer, Carlos, slouches across from her, fiddling with a loose thread on his rumpled suit jacket. His greasy hair is clinging to his scalp in uneven patches, and his yellowed teeth peek out as he chews on a toothpick.

"Miss O'Connor," he drawled, not bothering to look up from the folder he was half-heartedly flipping through. "We meet again."

"I need answers," Erin said firmly, though her voice wavered. "What's happening with my case?"

Carlos gave a lazy shrug. "Well, the good news is your boyfriend—sorry, *ex*-boyfriend—is awake." He flashed her a grin that didn't reach her eyes. "Fabio Silva, right? Seems to be making a full recovery."

Erin exhaled a breath she didn't realise she'd been holding. "He's awake? He's going to be okay, right?"

"Yes, yes," Carlos said dismissively, waving a hand as if Fabio's life was a minor detail. "The swelling has gone down, no permanent damage to his brain, according to his doctors."

For the first time in weeks, Erin feels a flicker of hope. If Fabio is recovering, then surely, he can clarify what really happened that night. He can tell the court it wasn't intentional, that she didn't mean to hurt him. Relief washes over her.

"That's good," she said, sitting forward in her chair. "Then he'll tell the truth, right? This can all be sorted out?"

Carlos snorted. "Sorted out? Sure, if you call a life sentence *sorted*."

Erin blinked, the colour draining from her face. "What do you mean? He knows I didn't mean to hit him. He knows I wouldn't—"

Carlos held up a hand, cutting her off. "Your dear Fabio isn't exactly singing your praises, Miss O'Connor. In fact, he's pushing for the harshest sentence possible. Attempted murder, he's calling it."

The words hit her like a physical blow.

She shook her head. "That's not true. He wouldn't—"

"Oh, he would," Carlos said with a sly grin. "And he is. Says you snapped that night, lost control, and ran him down on purpose. Claims you've always had a violent streak."

"That's a lie!" Erin snapped, her voice rising.

Carlos leaned back in his chair, unimpressed. "Well, it's his word against yours. And let's be honest, he's the one with a fractured skull. Makes for a pretty compelling victim, don't you think?"

Erin's fists clenched in her lap, her nails digging into her palms. "What about witnesses? Did anyone see what actually happened?"

"Nope," Carlos said, casually. "The only witnesses are people who saw you hit him. Not exactly in your favour, I'm afraid." He gave her a mock sympathetic look. "Tough break."

Her chest tightened, and she fought to steady her breathing. "You're supposed to be helping me. Defending me. But all you've done is tell me how hopeless it is."

Carlos sighed dramatically and leaned forward, resting his elbows on the table. "Look, Miss O'Connor, I'm not a miracle worker. You're a foreigner in a country with a legal system that doesn't favour outsiders. You're facing serious charges with flimsy evidence to back your story. And frankly—" He shrugged. "The odds aren't looking good."

"So that's it?" Erin demanded, her voice trembling with rage and despair. "You're just going to let them lock me up for something I didn't do?"

"Hey now," Carlos said, raising his hands in mock surrender. "Don't shoot the messenger. I'm doing what I can with what I've got. But let's be real—you're not exactly paying for top-notch representation here."

Erin's jaw tightened. "I didn't choose you. I can't afford to choose anyone else."

"Exactly," Carlos said, leaning back again. "So why don't we focus on damage control? Maybe we can argue for a reduced sentence if you play your cards right."

Her stomach churns. She feels trapped and suffocated by the indifference of the man who held her future in his hands.

That night, Erin lay on her cot, staring at the cracked ceiling of her cell. She replays Carlos's words over and over in her mind, each one a dagger to her fragile hope. Fabio's recovery has been her one lifeline; her belief that the truth would come to light. But now, that lifeline was fraying, and the darkness was closing in around her.

She thought of Fabio, of the man she once loved so deeply. The man who had made her laugh, who had held her close in the quiet hours of the night. How did it come to this? How has he become someone who would throw her to the wolves to save face?

A tear slides down her cheek, and she brushes it away angrily. She cannot afford to cry, not here. Not now.

The sound of footsteps echoes down the hallway, and Erin turns towards the bars of her cell. A guard passes by without a glance, the keys at his hip jangling with every step. She felt a pang of longing for the outside world, for freedom, for the life she has once known.

But freedom felt farther away than ever. As the walls of the cell close in around her, Erin realises that she is fighting a battle she isn't sure is even possible to win.

Over the next while, Carlos's visits became more infrequent, and his attitude remained as apathetic as ever. Erin's pleas for better representation went unanswered, her calls home are met with the same vague reassurances that her family is *working on it*.

Each time she picks up the phone, she hopes for a miracle—a sign that someone—anyone—is fighting for her. But the silence on the other end of the line speaks louder than words.

And as the days march on, Erin begins to understand the cruel reality of her situation. She is alone, trapped in a system that sees her as expendable. A pawn in a game she doesn't know how to play.

But she will not give up. Not yet anyway.

As the trial looms closer, Erin becomes hyperaware of her surroundings. Every noise, every glance from the guards, every whispered conversation between the other inmates feels significant, as though the entire prison is bracing for her departure.

The other women in her block give her a wide berth. Erin isn't sure if it is fear or pity, but either way, she is grateful for the distance. She cannot handle the forced cheer of small talk or the invasive questions about her case.

She spends most of her time hunched over the small, graffiti-covered desk in her cell, scribbling out lists of things she wishes she could say in court, though she knows she'll never be allowed to.

She writes letters to her family too, though she never sends them. What was the point? They won't respond.

The last two days before the trial are the worst. Erin feels like a woman walking towards the gallows, every step bringing her closer to an unknowable fate.

On the eve of the trial, she stays up late staring out the narrow window in her cell. The sky is dark, the stars faint against the glow of the city. She presses her hand to the cold glass, imagining she can see all the way to Tyrone. What is her family doing at that moment? Are they thinking of her?

Or have they already made their decision to stay home, turning the page on her as if she were a chapter best forgotten?

The guard comes to escort her to bed. "Big day tomorrow," he said with a smirk.

Erin didn't reply. She climbs into her cot, pulling the thin blanket up to her chin. She wonders if she'll wake up to find the courage to face the courtroom alone.

Or if she'll break entirely.

Chapter Five

The courtroom, humid and oppressively silent, feels miles away from the life Erin O'Connor once knew in Ireland. Beads of sweat cling to her forehead, trickling down her temple as the air seems to thicken with each passing second.

The smell of polished wood mingles with the faint, metallic tang of her shackles, and the dull hum of the ceiling fan above did little to alleviate the stifling heat. She sits alone at the defendant's table, shackled at the wrists; her only company is the guard station a step behind her.

Every scrape of a chair, every murmur among the onlookers, seems magnified in the stillness. Her heart thuds against her ribcage, a rhythm that drowns out the faint rustle of papers and the deliberate steps of the judge as he enters the room.

Erin's eyes roam the faces in the gallery, scanning for someone—anyone—familiar. But the rows of seats offer no solace. Not a single friend or family member has made the journey from Tyrone to Brazil to stand by her side. She knows it is unlikely, yet some small, desperate part of her holds on to the hope that a loved one walks through the doors.

That hope now crumbles, leaving a hollow ache in its wake. She can almost hear her mother's voice, sharp and unyielding, condemning her for the choices that had led her here. The distance between them was more than miles; it is an ocean of disappointment and estrangement, one that now feels insurmountable.

When Erin had first been arrested, she'd clung to the belief that her family would come. She'd imagined her father's quiet, steadfast presence. But as the trial unfolded, her hopes had withered.

Whether it was the expense, the shock of her alleged crime, or the pure embarrassment of it all, she would never know for sure. All she knew was that she faced this ordeal alone, with only her own words as evidence—words that now feel fragile and insufficient, like a thin sheet of ice over deep water.

Her thoughts snap back to the present as Fabio enters, his polished shoes clicking against the tiled floor. He takes the witness stand with a measured confidence that makes Erin's stomach twist.

Dressed impeccably in a dark suit, he looks every bit the picture of composure; his dark eyes scan the room before settling on her. She feels a cold stab of fear as their gazes meet.

He looks exactly as he did in those early days in Dublin: confident, controlled, that familiar intensity lingering in his gaze. For a moment, it was almost surreal, as if the years they'd spent together—and the violence of that night—were nothing but a dark fantasy.

Fabio clears his throat, his voice steady and deliberate as he begins to recount the events from his perspective. The words come smoothly, unbroken by hesitation. He paints a portrait of Erin, that is so far removed from who she thinks she is, that it leaves her breathless.

Fabio describes her as volatile and unpredictable, prone to violent outbursts. He tells the court how she had been drinking heavily that night, her behaviour growing more erratic until she'd snapped; deliberately running him down as he stood defenceless on the street.

The prosecutor steps forward, his tone crisp and deliberate. "Mr Silva, could you clarify for the court the nature of Ms O'Connor's behaviour leading up to the incident? What exactly did she say or do that evening?"

Fabio's brow furrows slightly, but his voice remains calm. "She…she was shouting, slurring her words. At first, it was arguments about something small—I don't even remember what. But then she started accusing me of…of things I hadn't done. Cheating, lying. She was…unstable."

"Unstable how?" the prosecutor pressed.

"She threw things. A glass, I think. She kept screaming that she hated me, that she'd make me regret everything. It wasn't the first time she'd acted like this, but that night was…worse."

Erin's lawyer, a wiry man with sharp features and a voice full of conviction, rises from his chair. "Objection, Your Honour. Speculation."

The judge, an older man with a lined face, nods slightly. "Sustained. Mr Silva, please, keep to what you directly observed."

Fabio nodded. "Yes, Your Honour. As I said, she was shouting and throwing things. I tried to leave the venue to get some space, but she followed me."

Erin's lawyer seizes the opportunity, stepping closer to the witness stand. "Mr Silva, you claim my client followed you, but isn't it true that earlier, witnesses reported hearing a heated argument where *you* were the one shouting? Isn't it true that your temper has been a point of contention in this relationship?"

Fabio's expression doesn't waver. "Yes, I raised my voice. But only because I was trying to get through to her. She was…she was out of control. I never laid a hand on her."

"Never?" Erin's lawyer's voice sharpened. "Would you like to explain why Ms O'Connor has photos of bruises and injuries, she claims you inflicted?"

Fabio shifts in his seat, his hands clasping the edge of the stand. "Those bruises weren't from me. She…she's clumsy. She'd trip, fall. She even admitted that once, didn't she?"

Erin's throat tightens as she fights the urge to shout. The truth seemed to dissolve in the air, replaced by the steady stream of his lies.

When Erin's lawyer begins cross-examining Fabio, there is a flicker of hope. He presses him on his own temper, his history of controlling behaviour, and his jealousy. But Fabio deflects with the ease of a seasoned actor, each denial as smooth as a polished stone.

He describes her as jealous, and possessive; painting a picture of a relationship fraught with tension and resentment—a stark contrast to the love she believed they shared. The life they had once built together now felt like a cruel joke, reframed to make her look like a monster.

Finally, the time comes for Erin to take the stand. Her heart is pounding so loudly that it drowns out the faint whispers in the gallery. She stands on trembling legs, shackles clinking softly as she makes her way to the witness box.

Her lawyer offers her a reassuring nod, but it does little to steady her nerves. She takes a deep breath and begins to speak, her voice shaky but determined.

She tells the court about the fear she had felt that night, the panic that took hold when Fabio's temper flared. She describes the way his words had cut like knives, the way his hands had gripped her arms with bruising force.

She explains how she acted out of self-preservation, not malice, and how the events of that night had spiralled out of her control. But as she speaks, she can see the doubt in the jurors' eyes and feel the weight of their scepticism pressing down on her.

Her voice wavers, betraying her nerves, and the prosecutor seizes on her uncertainty, twisting her words, poking holes in her account.

"Ms O'Connor," Fabio's lawyer—a tall man with a commanding presence and a cold, calculated smile—began smoothly. "You claim you were acting in self-defence. Yet the police report states that Mr Silva was standing several feet away from you when you struck him with the car. How do you explain that?"

Erin swallows hard; her palms slick against the wood of the witness box. "I—I wasn't thinking straight. I was scared. He'd been coming at me earlier, and I panicked."

"Panicked?" The lawyer's tone sharpened, cutting through her words. "Isn't it true, Ms O'Connor, that you had been drinking heavily that evening? That your judgment was impaired?"

"I...I had a drink," Erin admitted, her voice barely above a whisper. "But I wasn't drunk. I knew what was happening."

"Interesting," the lawyer said, pacing slightly. "So, you knew what was happening, but you chose to get behind the wheel of a vehicle and aim it at Mr Silva?"

"No!" Erin's voice cracked, her hands clutching the edges of the stand. "It wasn't like that! I wasn't aiming at him—I was trying to get away."

The lawyer stops and turns to face her, his eyes narrowing. "If you were trying to get away, Ms O'Connor, why didn't you call the police? Why didn't you seek help instead of taking matters into your own hands?"

Erin hesitates, her throat dry. "I...I didn't think I had time. I thought he'd—he'd catch me."

"Catch you?" The lawyer's voice dripped with scepticism. "And yet, here we have a man, severely injured, while you walked away without a scratch. Doesn't that seem...convenient?"

"Objection," Erin's lawyer interjected. "Argumentative."

The judge nodded. "Sustained. Mr DeSouza, please, rephrase."

Fabio's lawyer smirked slightly, turning back to Erin. "Let me ask you this, Ms O'Connor. If your actions were so justified, why is it that not a single family member has come here to support you? Surely, if you were the victim in this scenario, someone—anyone—would be here to stand by your side."

The words struck like a physical blow. Erin's vision blurring with tears as anger and humiliation bubbles to the surface.

"That doesn't mean anything!" she burst out, her voice rising. "They—they don't know the truth. They weren't there!"

"No," the lawyer said, his voice cold and deliberate. "They weren't there. But perhaps they know you better than we do. Perhaps they know you're capable of this."

"Enough!" Erin shouts, her fists pounding against the wood.

The courtroom gasps, murmurs rippling through the gallery. The judge bangs his gavel sharply.

"Order! Ms O'Connor, control yourself!"

Erin slumps back, her breathing ragged, her vision swimming. She feels the weight of every gaze in the room pressing down on her.

In the jury box, 12 faces are staring back at her, their expressions a mix of discomfort, doubt, and quiet judgment. One juror, a middle-aged woman with glasses perched on her nose, seemed to avoid Erin's eyes entirely.

Another, a younger man with a furrowed brow, leans forward slightly as if trying to catch every nuance. Erin wonders what they are thinking—if they see her as a victim or a villain, if they believe even a shred of her story.

The prosecutor stands, addressing the jury with a voice full of confidence. "Ladies and gentlemen, what we've seen today is a pattern—a pattern of violent, erratic behaviour. Mr Silva's testimony is consistent, credible and supported by evidence.

"And what do we see from Ms O'Connor? Contradictions, emotional outbursts, and a complete lack of support from those who know her best. Her own family hasn't come to her defence. Ask yourselves why."

Erin's lawyer rose, his voice quieter but firm. "Members of the jury, I urge you to look beyond the surface. My client has admitted her fear, her panic and her humanity. Does that make her guilty of attempted murder?

"Or does it make her someone who acted out of terror, someone who felt she had no other choice? Consider the bruises on her arms and the reports of Fabio Silva's temper. This isn't as simple as the prosecution would have you believe."

As the closing arguments conclude, Erin sits frozen, staring at the wood grain of the defence table, numb and exhausted. She tries to absorb the reality of what lay before her, the heavy weight of the jury's deliberation. Hours pass, or maybe it was only minutes before they return with the verdict: *Guilty of attempted murder.*

The words crash over her, sending a ripple of shock through the courtroom. She feels herself go numb as the judge continues, his words are a droning murmur as he sentences her to life in a maximum-security prison. Life.

The finality of it echoes in her mind; a crushing weight that seems to close off any hope of redemption, any possibility of ever returning to the life she had once dreamed of.

As she is escorted out of the courtroom, she risks one last glance at Fabio. He is watching her, his face expressionless at first, his gaze impassive and unreadable. She searches his eyes for something—remorse, regret, even a hint of responsibility.

And then, as she is crossing the threshold to her new life, she catches it. A slight smirk appears on the corner of his mouth, a victory smile of sorts. And that was that.

Chapter Six

The journey back to the prison feels endless. Outside the windows of the transport van, the landscape of Brazil passes by—vibrant and alive—oblivious to Erin's suffering. Towering palms sway in the warm breeze, their vibrant green contrasting sharply with the endless blue of the sky.

Tiny villages dot the countryside, where children play and adults go about their daily routines, unaware of the despair hidden within the van's metal walls. Erin wants to scream, to cry out, to claw her way out of this nightmare, but all she can manage is a faint, guttural whimper.

The realisation that her life is about to get unimaginably worse weighs down on her chest like a slab of concrete. Each bump in the road jostles her shackled wrists and ankles, the metal biting into her skin. The other women in the van sit in heavy silence, their faces a mix of exhaustion and resignation. Erin caught fleeting glances from some of them—curious, assessing and pitying all at once. She hates it. She wants to look strong, to exude some semblance of control, but the fear bubbling inside her makes her hands tremble uncontrollably. The finality of her transfer becomes clearer with each passing kilometre. The temporary holding facility she has left now felt like a distant paradise in comparison to what lies ahead. It hadn't been ideal, but at least, there had been some semblance of order, a routine she could navigate without constant terror. This new prison, however, was infamous. Its reputation had seeped into her consciousness long before she'd even stepped foot in Brazil. A hellish fortress of fear and brutality. It was a place where survival depended solely on alliances and strength.

Rumours of gang wars, merciless hierarchies and unchecked violence churn in her mind. The prison transport van finally slows, rumbling over gravel roads. Erin's heart sinks further as towering walls crowned with coils of razor wire come into view. This is it.

The van passes through multiple gates, each heavier and more foreboding than the last until they reach the final barrier. Guard towers loom above, manned by officers with rifles slung over their shoulders; their sharp eyes scanning the area for any sign of trouble.

Yet, it wasn't the guards who maintain order within those walls—that was left to the inmates themselves. Ruled by the gangs that held dominion over the prison's sprawling yard and cell blocks.

As the van comes to a halt and the doors swing open, a cacophony of jeers and shouts erupt from a crowd of inmates. They press themselves against the chain-link fence that separates the intake area from the general yard. Erin feels the heat of their eyes boring into her, and their voices laced with mockery and cruel anticipation.

She has never felt so exposed. The air is thick with hostility, and the sound of their laughter echoes like a sinister promise. Erin hesitates, her shackled feet reluctant to move, but a prison guard begins to bark orders in Portuguese, shoving her forward with the blunt end of their baton.

She shuffles out, her head held high in an attempt to mask her fear, but the weight of the inmates' stares bear down on her. It is as though she is an animal being released into an arena, surrounded by predators eager for new blood. She steals a glance at the other women being processed beside her. Some of them stare straight ahead, their faces blank masks of indifference. Others exchange nervous glances, their hands trembling as they clutch the meagre belongings they are permitted to bring. Erin envies their silence, their ability to keep their emotions hidden.

Her own fear is written all over her face, and she knows it. Inside the intake building, the process is quick and impersonal. Erin is handed a thin, ill-fitting prison uniform—a drab grey that matches the hopelessness she feels inside. Two sheets of paper were thrust at her: one printed with basic rules and the other a map of the prison layout.

The rules seem almost laughable; she has already heard enough to know they were nothing more than empty words. Here, the law is made and enforced by the inmates, not the guards. The guards, indifferent and silent, don't bother to explain anything.

They move like automatons, their eyes glazed with boredom as they go through the motions. They are there to process, not protect. Erin caught snippets of whispered conversations between other inmates as they waited—rumours of beatings, extortion, and the gangs that rule the prison with an iron fist.

She clenches the papers in her hands so tightly that they crumple. When the final gate opens, the guard's step aside, leaving her to walk into the main yard alone. The clang of the metal door slamming shut behind her sends a jolt of panic through her chest.

The yard is vast and chaotic, a concrete expanse littered with makeshift benches, tables and crude exercise equipment. Groups of women cluster together, their postures territorial. Many are covered in tattoos, and intricate patterns that wound their way across their arms, necks, and faces.

Others bore scars, both old and fresh, their skin a patchwork of violence. Erin tries to walk with purpose, but every step feels heavier than the last. She can't help but notice how the inmates move in tight-knit packs, like wolves guarding their turf. Each group occupies its own section of the yard, the lines of demarcation invisible but deeply understood.

She can feel their eyes following her, assessing her, cataloguing her weaknesses. A few women leer openly, their smiles predatory. Erin fights the urge to shrink under their gaze, forcing herself to keep her head high. The last thing she can afford to show is fear, but it is there in every shaky breath she takes.

In the distance, a fight breaks out between two women, their screams cutting through the oppressive heat. No one rushes to stop it—not the guards perched on the exterior walls, and certainly not the other inmates.

A circle quickly forms around the combatants, the crowd cheering and shouting as punches land with sickening thuds. Erin turns away, her stomach churning. It doesn't take her long to understand the unspoken rules of this place. Survival isn't just about physical strength—it is about alliances, cunningness, and the ability to adapt.

She realises with a sinking heart that she has no one here. No allies. No protection. She is on her own in a world where weakness is a death sentence. As she moves, she can feel eyes tracking her every step. New inmates are fresh targets; vulnerable in their lack of alliances and known to be easier to manipulate, humiliate or simply brutalise.

She barely makes it a few yards before she is approached by two women. They are both older, scarred from what looked like years of survival in this unforgiving place. Without a word, one of them shoves her hard enough to send her stumbling backwards. She hears the dull thud of laughter around her as she steadies herself, the air thick with menace.

"What's the matter, gringa? Lost your way?" the taller woman sneered, her accent sharp and mocking.

"Just trying to stay out of trouble," Erin said, her voice steady but low.

The response is met with a laugh, and the other woman steps forward, curling her fingers around Erin's hair and yanks her head back. She can smell the stale breath of her assailant as she whispers in her ear.

"Oh, you'll find trouble here. Or it'll find you."

They release her, but the message is clear: she is the prey here, and any sign of weakness will be exploited. Erin stumbles back, swallowing her pride and anger as she moves deeper into the yard. Her mind spins with how she is going to make it through even one day, let alone a lifetime.

Chapter Seven

In the days that follow, Erin is subjected to a relentless barrage of harassment. It begins subtly—a shove in the yard, a mocking laugh as she passes, cruel whispers exchanged just loud enough for her to hear. But soon, it escalates.

She is tripped deliberately in the crowded hallways, her knees scraping against the filthy floors, and shoved hard enough to bruise her arms on the jagged edges of the walls. Even during meals, when everyone else seems too preoccupied with securing their food, she isn't spared.

A sneering inmate spills water on her lap, another swipes her bread roll with a look of mocking satisfaction. Every incident is a test, a way of gauging her reaction. No matter how much she tries to avoid confrontation, it seems to invite more.

It becomes clear that every new inmate has to prove themselves one way or another. There is no escape from the gauntlet of cruelty that greets fresh arrivals.

In a place where no official hierarchy exists, brutality is the currency of respect, and Erin finds herself coming up woefully short. Her quiet demeanour and refusal to retaliate marks her as weak; a target for those eager to assert their dominance.

Her nights offer no reprieve. The cells are cramped and sweltering, with barely enough space to lie down. Her cellmate—a brooding woman with a face like stone—doesn't speak much but watches Erin's every move with a cold, predatory intensity.

Beyond their cell walls, the sounds of the prison are unrelenting. Shouting, cursing, and the occasional chilling scream echoes endlessly through the block; a cruel reminder of the violence that lurks around every corner.

Sleep comes in fractured moments, if at all. Erin lies on the thin, stained mattress. Her body tense and coiled like a spring, her mind unable to settle. Every creak of the cell door, every shuffling footstep, sends her heart racing as she braces for an attack that never comes—at least not yet.

The bruises on her arms and legs multiply, each one a silent testament to the war of attrition being waged against her. Slowly but surely, the prison is stripping her down, leaving her raw and vulnerable.

The worst encounter comes one morning while waiting in line for breakfast. Erin is standing quietly, her eyes on the floor as she shuffles forward, and a sharp shove from behind sends her staggering into the woman ahead of her.

Before she can steady herself or even apologise, a fist collides with her jaw, snapping her head to the side with a sickening crack.

The world tilts for a moment as Erin stumbles back, her vision swimming. Her hand flew to her face, her fingers trembling as they brush against her throbbing jaw. The taste of copper fills her mouth as she realises her lip is bleeding.

The yard seems to freeze around her, the usual din of conversations and clattering trays are replaced by the low hum of murmured excitement. A circle is forming, and Erin finds herself at its centre; her attacker standing over her with a grin that was equal parts amusement and menace.

The woman is tall and solidly built, her muscular arms are covered in tattoos that twist and coiled like snakes. She is clearly someone important; a gang enforcer if the respect in the eyes of the onlookers is any indication.

Erin feels a chill run down her spine as she realises that this isn't just an attack—it is an initiation of sorts, a brutal ritual designed to test her mettle.

The enforcer steps forward, her fists raised, and Erin's instincts begin to kick in. Gritting her teeth against the pain radiating from her jaw, she raises her own fists, ready to defend herself. But before she can throw a single punch, the woman strikes again, her fist sinking into Erin's stomach with precision.

The air is forced from her lungs in a single, agonising gasp, and Erin doubles over, clutching her abdomen. Another blow lands against her ribs, sending her sprawling onto the gravel-covered ground.

The sharp stones bite into her skin, and she grits her teeth against the sting as she struggles to push herself up. But before she can, a boot connects with her side, rolling her onto her back with a force that leaves her winded.

Above her, the enforcer looms like a shadow, her smile widening as she prepares for another strike. Around them, the crowd erupts into cheers and jeers, their voices a cacophony of cruelty that fills Erin's ears.

But beneath the pain and humiliation, something stirs within her. It is small at first, a flicker of defiance buried deep in her chest. They want her to cower, to beg, to break—but she won't. She can't.

As she lay there, staring up at her attacker through the blur of her tears, Erin makes a silent promise to herself: she will survive this place, no matter what it takes.

That promise becomes a lifeline in the days that follow. Survival means adapting and learning to navigate the dangerous social landscape of the prison. Erin quickly realises that she will have to form alliances, no matter how much she loathes the idea. Being a lone wolf in this environment is as good as signing her own death warrant.

She observes the factions carefully, noting how they operate and who holds the most power. The gangs are territorial, their members fiercely loyal and unforgiving of betrayal.

Every act of kindness or solidarity comes with strings attached—a price that will eventually be called in. Erin hates the idea of owing anyone, but she knows that her pride has no place here.

The violence doesn't stop, but Erin begins to change. She becomes sharper, quicker, her instincts honing by the unending threat of danger. She learns to anticipate attacks, to read the body language of those around her, and to strike first when necessary. The bruises and scars continue to accumulate, but so does her resolve.

One afternoon, as she sits in the yard nursing a particularly nasty bruise on her cheek, a woman approaches her. She is older and wiry, with a face lined by years of hardship. Her dark eyes were sharp and calculating, and Erin could tell immediately that she is someone who had survived this place for a long time.

The woman introduces herself as Ana and offers Erin a cigarette; a gesture that seems impossibly generous in a place where kindness is rare. They smoke in silence for a while, the acrid smoke curling into the humid air.

Then Ana leans closer, her voice low and conspiratorial. "It's about to get a lot worse for you, gringa," she murmurs. "You'll need people here, whether you like it or not. Alone? You won't last."

The words stay with Erin long after Ana walks away. As much as she hates to admit it, Ana is right. Survival here isn't just about strength—it is about strategy, about playing the game, but Erin just isn't ready to offer herself to a gang.

She will continue to go solo for now, but she can't ignore the changes within herself. The girl who once dreamed of love and freedom—who believed in the goodness of people—is fading. In her place is someone harder, colder—a woman getting shaped by the darkness of this place.

She isn't sure if she will ever find her way back to the person, she once was. But for now, survival is all that matters. Deep down, beneath the layers of anger and fear, Erin clung to a tiny, flickering hope, that one day, she will escape this nightmare and reclaim the pieces of herself that the prison haven't yet stolen.

Chapter Eight

One morning, Erin is jolted awake by the sound of her cell door slamming open. Groggy and still sore from the relentless grind of the previous days, she blinks rapidly, trying to make sense of what is happening.

Her heart races when she realises her small cell is filled with around 10 inmates, all of them are seasoned veterans of this brutal world. Their presence isn't casual or random—it carries purpose. They don't speak, but their expressions tell her everything she needs to know.

This isn't a routine hazing, nor one of the spontaneous attacks she'd endured since her arrival. This is different.

The largest of the group, a woman with short-cropped hair and tattoos crawling up her neck, gestures for Erin to get up. Her voice, though calm, carries an authority that demands compliance.

"Levanta," she said. "Get up."

Erin's body moves on instinct, her muscles tense as she swings her legs over the side of the cot. Her mind is overloaded, piecing together fragments of Ana's cryptic warnings.

"It's about to get a lot worse for you, gringa."

Ana tried to prepare her, in her own way, but she had never told Erin what exactly to expect. Now, it is all becoming horrifyingly clear.

The group surrounds her in a loose formation as they march her out of the cell block. Erin keeps her head down, her heart pounding in her chest. The hallway feels longer than usual, the walls narrowing as her anxiety grows. She can feel the eyes of other prisoners on her as they pass. Whispers follow in their wake, carrying on a current of grim anticipation.

They don't take her to the usual yard. Instead, they led her to an inconspicuous metal door embedded in what she'd always assume is the outer boundary of the prison. The door is small and nondescript, almost invisible against the aged concrete walls. Two guards flank it, their expressions unreadable as they unlock it and step aside.

Erin hesitates for a moment, but a sharp shove from one of the inmates pushes her forward. She stumbles through the door, squinting as the sunlight hits her face.

What lay beyond made her stomach drop.

This isn't the familiar yard she has grown accustomed to. It is a hidden area, surrounded by high walls that are even more imposing than the ones enclosing the rest of the prison. In the centre of the space is a makeshift ring—roughly marked off by ropes strung between poles hammered into the ground. The dirt around the ring is hard-packed and stained in places, hinting at the grim history of this place.

Around the ring stands a crowd. Erin immediately notices the hierarchy within it. At the forefront are gang members, their postures casual but their eyes sharp, sizing her up.

Behind them are other seasoned prisoners, those who had earned the privilege of spectating such an event. And then, beyond them, scattered along the edges of the yard, are the prison guards.

The guards' presence chills Erin to her core. They aren't here to maintain order. They are here to watch. Their indifference to the violence within the prison walls had always been unsettling, but this is something else entirely.

Some lean against the walls with cigarettes in hand, while others chat amongst themselves, barely glancing at her as she is brought closer to the ring.

Erin doesn't need to speak perfect Portuguese to understand what is happening. The roars of the crowd, the jeers, and the sharp clang of a bell tells her all she needs to know. She is about to fight.

She looks over her shoulder, searching for Ana, hoping for some kind of reassurance. Ana stands at the edge of the crowd, her face expressionless, but her eyes portray a flicker of regret. It is clear now that Ana knows this moment was coming, but there had been no way to stop it.

The realisation hits Erin like a blow to the head. All the hazing, the random attacks, the relentless beatings—they hadn't been arbitrary. They were preparing her for this day.

The inmates were testing her endurance, conditioning her to survive in a place where weakness is a death sentence. And now, they will be able to tell if she has learned enough to endure the real test.

On the blood-soaked grounds of the secret prison yard, Erin finds herself thrust into a world of savage survival that defies belief. Here, the brutality transcends mere hostility or petty rivalry; it has been institutionalised into a sick spectacle.

A twisted sport where prisoners, especially new ones, are forced to fight each other in bare-knuckle brawls to the finish.

The fights aren't overseen by referees or controlled by rules. Instead, they're brutal tests of endurance, with victory declared only when one fighter genuinely can't get up or is rendered unconscious. It is not uncommon for inmates to die out on the makeshift ring within the prison yard.

It's a cycle without mercy or reprieve, and the stakes of each fight are more than life or death for the women forced into the ring. Outside the fight circle, drugs, cigarettes, scraps of food, and even essential supplies like sanitary pads are wagered on each match.

The betting is merciless, with inmates and even prison guards staking whatever they can on the spectacle of survival. In this hellish colosseum, Erin finds herself the subject of grim amusement, with no place to hide and no way to opt-out.

Across the ring, her opponent steps forward. The woman is taller and broader, with an air of calm menace that speaks of experience. Her hands are taped, her knuckles scarred from countless fights. She looks Erin over with the detached confidence of someone who has done this many times before.

As the fight gets underway, Erin struggles to keep her balance in this vicious new routine. She stumbles slightly as her opponent pushes her onto the packed dirt. Her legs feel unsteady, her body screaming in protest from the countless injuries she has accumulated.

The prison guards, with cigarettes dangling from their lips, are placing bets on which woman will go down first. Their faces are blank, almost bored, as if this is merely a part of their daily routine. They are as much spectators as the inmates themselves, but their cold detachment only deepens the sense of despair that fills the air.

In this place, no one will step in to break up a fight or call for mercy. The guards will watch a woman be beaten to within an inch of her life, and if she dies, they'll shrug and move on.

The crowd grows louder as the two women trade blows. The gang members exchange bets, tossing cigarettes, food, and other contraband into piles at their feet.

Erin clenches her fists, forcing herself to steady her breathing.

"You've been through worse," she tells herself, though she isn't sure if it is true.

The weeks of surviving in the prison yard, of enduring the relentless beatings and hazing, had been a kind of training.

She has learned to take hits, to read her opponent's movements, and to stay on her feet even when her body begs her to fall.

The crowd again erupts in cheers and taunts, their voices a cacophony that blurred together in Erin's ears.

As the fight goes on, Erin begins to adapt. She sidesteps a wild swing, her opponent's fist grazing her cheek instead of landing squarely. The small victory gives her a surge of confidence, and she counters with a clumsy punch of her own. It isn't enough to do much damage, but it is enough to show the crowd that she isn't entirely defenceless.

The fight becomes a blur of motion and pain, the world narrowing to the sound of her own heartbeat and the relentless rhythm of strikes and dodges.

Erin didn't know how long it lasted, but by the time it was over, her body was bruised and trembling, her breath coming in ragged gasps. Her opponent is down, blood dripping from a split lip. A hard-faced gang leader with a notepad gives Erin a curt nod to exit the ring.

The crowd begins to disperse, the energy in the yard shifting as the spectators move on to whatever comes next. Erin sinks to her knees; the dirt feels cool against her palms. She feels a hand on her shoulder and looks up to see Ana, her expression still unreadable.

"You made it through," Ana said quietly. "That's what matters."

But as Erin looks around the yard, at the gang members counting their winnings and the guards lighting fresh cigarettes, she knows this wasn't her last fight.

Her follow-up fights are just as brutal. Her opponents are often seasoned women, those who have hardened into ruthless fighters after years in the prison system. These women fight not just for survival but for dominance, for whatever scraps of power the prison yard allows.

For Erin, each beating is a harsh, relentless initiation into a world where her own life reduces to a sick form of entertainment. She learns fast that the only way to avoid worse treatment is to keep getting up; to stand on legs that shake with exhaustion and fists that tremble with barely contained pain.

The physical toll on Erin is immense. Every fight leaves her more bruised and battered. Her body became a patchwork of purples and greens, cuts and swollen flesh. There is no infirmary here, no place to tend to her injuries or recuperate from the beatings she endures.

She wakes each day with her body screaming in pain, yet there's no choice but to push forward, knowing she'll be called upon to fight again before she's even remotely healed.

Recovery is a luxury she isn't afforded, and there are days when her only wish is that she doesn't wake up at all.

She finds herself praying for some kind of release. Her spirit is slowly being worn down by the relentless grind of the fights, the jeering crowds, and the unforgiving brutality of her new reality.

Each fight is a battle against, not only her opponent, but also against her own despair. The beatings are so frequent and vicious that Erin begins to lose count of how many times she's been forced into the dirt. How many times she's been beaten to the point where she can't remember what day it is or even who she was before she entered this place.

At times, the urge to surrender—to simply stay down, close her eyes, and let the darkness swallow her whole—becomes overpowering. But somehow, something within her refuses to give up entirely. There's a stubborn flicker of defiance buried deep within, a spark that keeps her going even when she feels she has nothing left.

Erin's growing endurance, however, does not escape the notice of others in the yard. The seasoned inmates watch her with a mixture of amusement and begrudging respect as she repeatedly pulls herself up from the ground after each beating, her eyes glazing with pain but unwavering.

Her resilience becomes something of a curiosity, and gradually, she senses that her willingness to endure might be her only weapon here. She doesn't have the skill or strength of some of the hardened fighters, but she has a kind of grit that, she realises, might be her key to survival.

But as her tolerance grows, so does the harshness of the fights she's forced into. The prison enforcers—those who organise these brutal displays for profit and amusement—

begin setting her up with tougher opponents; women twice her size or those known for their ruthlessness. It's as if they're testing her limits, watching to see when she'll finally break.

In one especially gruelling fight, Erin faces an opponent who is another known enforcer, a woman with a reputation for violence and a history of leaving her victims bloodied and broken. The crowd cheers as the woman strides forward, her fists are already clenched, and her eyes alight with a brutal kind of joy.

For Erin, the fight is a familiar blur of pain and desperation. Each blow drives her closer to the edge, her vision darkening, her body too exhausted to respond. But when she's knocked to the ground, she manages to drag herself back up, spitting blood and glaring defiantly, even as her body screams for her to stay down.

Somehow, she survives—barely—but the price is steep. Her body is wracked with injuries, her spirit is pushed to its breaking point.

As the days bleed into each other, Erin finds herself growing numb to the violence, her mind and body adapting in ways she never thought possible. She learns to anticipate the rhythm of the fights and to brace herself for impact. Also, to summon a detached calm that allows her to keep going even when every instinct tells her to give up.

The despair that once threatened to overwhelm her, begins to harden into something colder, something that feels almost like determination. In the depths of this brutal existence, she discovers a core of resilience she never knew she had—a stubborn refusal to let this place consume her completely.

The jeers and taunts of the crowd become background noise, a constant hum of cruelty that she learns to ignore. The pain becomes familiar, a part of her daily reality, and she stops thinking of escape or rescue.

In this place, survival is a battle she fights alone, and each day that she manages to stay alive is a small victory; a quiet act of defiance against the prison that seeks to break her.

The brutality, however, is unending. Erin's hope flickers dimly, often nearly extinguished, but somewhere in the depths of her heart, a quiet rage smoulders, fuelling her resolve.

She realises that if she is going to survive, she can't just endure—she'll need to fight back, not just against her opponents in the yard but against the prison itself, against the hopelessness that threatens to consume her.

And as she walks towards yet another fight—her fists clenched, and her body battered—she feels that glimmer of defiance grows stronger. She may be bruised, broken and exhausted, but she is still alive—still standing. And in this place, she is adamant that no one can take that from her.

Chapter Nine

The relentless cycle of violence and despair that Erin has endured begins to take an unexpected turn. Battered and emotionally numbed by the prison's brutal system, she has long resigned herself to the daily grind of fights, jeers, and the aching loneliness that accompanies them.

Each day blurs into the next; a survival game where the stakes are her body, her mind, and what remains of her dignity. But today is different. Today, the unbroken monotony fractures, letting in a sliver of something unfamiliar—attention.

Erin has always flown under the radar, a figure on the periphery of the prison's power dynamics. The weak don't last long here, and the strong seldom waste their time with anyone who doesn't serve their interests.

Yet, as she stumbles away from her latest fight, her face bloodied and her body screaming in protest, she senses a change. Dragging herself to her corner of the yard, she tries to ignore the throbbing in her side and the now familiar taste of copper in her mouth.

She expects to be left alone, as always, to patch herself up with trembling hands and the frayed hem of her shirt. But this time, she isn't alone.

Instead, she finds herself at the centre of some quiet, curious attention from a group of inmates she's seen only from the sidelines until now. Known as the *Irmandade*, this gang is one of the most powerful in the prison. It is rumoured to control not only the fighting circuit but much of the black-market trade within the prison walls.

They are not just a gang; they are a force of nature. Feared and respected in equal measure, a shadowy family bound together by loyalty and shared survival; they've taken notice of Erin's resilience.

From the edge of her vision, she sees three women approaching. Their faces are stern and unreadable, and she steels herself for another assault.

The leader of the group, a wiry woman with sharp eyes and a scar running across her cheek, gestures for Erin to follow. Her voice is calm but commanding, giving Erin no choice but to obey.

The group leads her to a quieter part of the yard, away from the prying eyes of the other prisoners and guards. There, they sit her down, offering her water and some makeshift bandages for her wounds.

The woman introduces herself as Rosa, a senior figure in the Irmandade. She's tough and no-nonsense, her face is weathered by years of life in prison, but there's an unmistakable glint of intelligence and strength in her eyes.

Rosa explains that they've been watching Erin ever since she arrived, observing her determination, and her ability to withstand pain, and also to continuously come back from each beating with a look of defiance. This resilience has earned Erin a measure of respect from the gang—a rare thing in a place where weakness is often met with exploitation or violence.

Rosa leans forward, her voice low but direct. "You've survived this long on guts alone," she says, "but guts won't be enough if you want to last in here. You need skill. Strategy. Someone to teach you how to win, without inflicting as much pain on yourself."

Erin, still cautious but desperate for anything that might help her survive, agrees to their offer. This moment marks a significant shift in her life within the prison. For the first time, she feels something beyond fear or dread.

The Irmandade's members treat her wounds with care. They instruct her on how to wrap her hands for protection and guide her through breathing exercises to ease the pain from her injuries.

What follows is nothing short of transformative. Over the next few weeks, Erin trains under the Irmandade's tutelage. Rosa teaches her the art of endurance: how to conserve her energy in a fight and strike with precision. Marisol, a towering woman with hands like iron, shows her how to strengthen her grip and build her stamina.

Talia, the smallest of the group but arguably the most dangerous, introduces her to the psychology of combat: how to read an opponent's intentions, exploit their weaknesses, and stay one step ahead.

The training is brutal but effective. They push Erin to her limits, forcing her to confront the fear and doubt that have plagued her since her imprisonment. Slowly, she begins to change. Her movements become sharper, her strikes more calculated. She learns to anticipate her opponents and to see openings where before she saw only chaos.

Erin gains something far more valuable than just physical skills: a sense of belonging. The women of the Irmandade are not gentle—life here has stripped them of softness—but their rough camaraderie fills a void Erin hasn't realised is so deep.

They share their stories with her, tales of loss, betrayal and survival. They teach her, not just how to fight but how to endure, and how to channel her pain into strength. They teach her where to strike to do maximum damage with minimal effort; how to stay balanced on her feet, and how to use her surroundings to her advantage.

Erin learns that in this place, fighting is as much a mental game as it is physical. She must maintain control, stay focused, and keep her fear in check.

As Erin trains with them, she learns to trust again, and she starts to bond with the women who have taken her under their wing. They are fierce, protective, and, in a strange way, maternal towards her.

They see in her someone who has endured suffering and survived, and they recognise the potential for strength beneath her bruised and battered exterior.

For the first time since her imprisonment, Erin starts to feel like she has allies. The Irmandade may not be friends in the traditional sense. They are hardened by the brutal world they live in, and their camaraderie is tinged with a mutual understanding of each other's darkness.

But they give her something invaluable: knowledge, protection, and a sense of identity beyond victimhood.

Their guidance transforms her. She no longer stumbles into the ring unprepared, nor does she allow her opponents to dominate her without a fight. Under their instruction, she learns to move with purpose and to strike with confidence.

She becomes quicker, sharper, and more aware of her own strengths and weaknesses.

When the time comes for her next fight, Erin is no longer the frightened newcomer who stumbles her way into survival. She's equipped with skills and strategies, bolstered by the knowledge that she has allies watching her back.

Erin's transformation does not go unnoticed by the other prisoners. She gains a reputation as someone who isn't easy to intimidate; a fighter with ferocity and endurance who commands respect.

The gang's protection shields her from much of the casual violence that new inmates often face, and she begins to walk the prison grounds with her head held higher; no longer shrinking from the menacing stares of other inmates.

This newfound strength, however, comes at a cost. The fights are still brutal, and there are still times when she comes away from the ring bloodied and barely able to stand. But now, she is fighting not just for survival but to prove herself—to honour the trust and faith her new *family* has placed in her.

Each fight, each bruise and each small victory is a testament to her resilience and the strength she has found in this unlikely alliance.

As the weeks pass, Erin realises that the Irmandade has given her something she thought she had lost forever: hope. Their camaraderie and their belief in her, has reignited a spark within her; a quiet but unyielding determination to survive, no matter the odds.

The friendships she forms with Rosa, Marisol and Talia become the closest thing to family she's known in years. A bond forged in the crucible of shared suffering and hard-won survival.

In this brutal place, surrounded by violence and despair, Erin has found her own strength, and with it, a fierce loyalty to the women who have helped her rise. The Irmandade's protection and mentorship have given her not only the means to endure but also the hope that she might one day be able to fight her way towards freedom.

Erin has a renewed resolve as she walks back to her cell after another gruelling day, her body aching but her heart filled with quiet pride. She has found a purpose, a family, and a way to survive—and she knows now that she is no longer alone in this battle.

As long as she has the Irmandade by her side, she feels that maybe, just maybe, she can endure anything that this place throws at her.

Chapter Ten

Erin O'Connor lay on the creaking prison cot, the ceiling above her little more than a mass of peeling paint and faint water stains. The clamour of the cellblock barely registers—she is far away, lost in the folds of her memory.

She let herself drift back to the one time in her life when she'd felt truly free. A summer when the world had seemed brighter and bigger than the limits of Tyrone.

The Gaeltacht in Gweedore, or Gaoth Dobhair as the locals called it, was a strange and magical place to Erin when she first arrived at the tender age of 15. Until then, she'd been shackled by a quiet shyness that coloured her interactions with everyone she met.

The countryside in Tyrone was a small world, and in that world, Erin had been an afterthought—a quiet, polite girl who never raised her hand too high or her voice above a murmur.

When her mother had suggested the summer immersion program in the Irish-speaking region, Erin had been both terrified and exhilarated. For once, she stepped outside the narrow boundaries of her small village. And maybe—just maybe—she might find something out there that was missing inside her.

The moment she stepped off the bus in Gweedore, she felt as though she'd landed on a different planet. The sea stretched out in the distance, endless and shimmering under the Donegal sunlight. Mountains loomed on the horizon, rugged and untamed. The air smelled of salt and heather, a far cry from the damp and earthy scents of home.

The first week was tough. Erin had been assigned to stay with a local bean an tí, an older woman named Máire who ran a traditional Irish-speaking home. Máire had strict rules about speaking only in Irish, and Erin stumbled over her words constantly.

Her face turned red with embarrassment every time Máire gently corrected her. The other teenagers in the program seemed to have no such trouble. They were outgoing, confident and loud—a stark contrast to Erin, who spent most of her time observing rather than participating.

Then came the first Céilí.

Máire dragged all the students to the local hall, where the lilting notes of a fiddle and the rhythmic stomps of feet filled the air. Erin had pressed herself into a corner, wishing she could disappear into the wooden walls. But that's when she first met Callum.

Callum McBride was tall, with a mop of unruly dark hair and a mischievous grin that made it seem like he was always on the verge of laughing at a private joke.

"You can't hide all night," he'd said to her, his Donegal accent was thick and warm.

Before she could protest, he'd taken her hand and pulled her into the crowd.

The first few minutes were awkward. Erin was stumbling over the steps of the traditional dances and constantly trying to break away and leave the floor, but Callum was patient.

"You're a fighter," he said when she tried to duck out, her face burning with mortification. "I can see it. Now stop thinking so much and just go with the music. Don't fight against it, just go with the flow."

By the end of the night, she was laughing, her feet moving in time with the jigs and reels. It was the first time she'd felt seen—really seen—in years or maybe ever.

Over the next few weeks, Erin found herself transforming. Her new group of friends—Callum, Aoife, Niamh, and a few others—welcomed her in without hesitation. They spent their days learning Irish in the classroom and their evenings exploring the wild beauty of Gweedore.

Erin learned to climb rocks along the coast, her hands raw but her spirit soaring. She dared to swim in the icy Atlantic, shrieking with laughter as the waves crashed over her.

She began to notice that her friends treated her differently as the summer wore on. They teased her, yes, but always in a way that felt affectionate, never cruel. They called her Bad Erin. It was a nickname born out of her unexpected willingness to tackle every challenge thrown her way.

The name had been inspired by the local landmark known as Bad Eddie, the skeleton of an old shipwreck beached on the sands of Gweedore. Erin had been fascinated by it from the moment she saw it; the way it stood defiantly against the elements, a testament to resilience.

"You're not unlike that old wreck," Callum told her one evening as they sat on the beach, watching the sun dip below the horizon. "Stronger than you look. Stubborn for sure. A born survivor."

Callum, with his endless supply of stories and folklore, became her closest friend that summer. He seemed to know every tale about the region, from the banshee that haunted the hills to the selkies that slipped between sea and shore.

But his favourite story was about two young sisters around their own age, who had fought off British soldiers during the Anglo-Norman invasion.

"They were just two kids," he said one evening, his voice hushed as they sat around a crackling fire. "But they had guts. Boiling water, stolen shotguns—they used whatever they had to protect what was theirs. They didn't back down, no matter how impossible it seemed."

Erin hung on every word; her chest tightened with an emotion she couldn't quite name. There was something about the story that resonated with her, something that made her sit up a little straighter, and hold her head a little higher.

"You remind me of them," Callum said, catching her off guard.

"Me?" she scoffed, shaking her head.

"Yeah. You've got that same fire. You just don't know it yet."

By the time the summer drew to a close, Erin barely recognised herself. She was no longer the timid girl who had arrived in Gweedore with her head bowed and her voice barely above a whisper. She was Bad Erin now, a nickname that started as a joke but had come to mean so much more. She was bold. She was brave. She was alive.

On the last night, her friends had surprised her with a gift—a Donegal GAA football jersey. It was too big for her, the fabric hanging loose around her frame, but she'd worn it proudly. Tears started pricking her eyes as they told her it was a reminder of who she'd become.

"A brave fighter," Callum had said, his voice soft but certain.

As Erin lay on her prison cot, the memory of that summer washed over her like a wave. She could almost hear the laughter of her friends, the crash of the sea, the haunting notes of a fiddle carried on the wind. Her chest ached with longing.

In Gweedore, she had discovered a version of herself she hadn't known existed. A version she thinks she has lost somewhere along the way. Erin lay and smile for what seem like an eternity.

But as the memory fades and is replaced by the cold reality of her cell, she clings to one thought: *Bad Erin isn't gone*. She is still here, buried under layers of pain and regret, but she is here.

And she isn't done fighting yet.

Chapter Eleven

Erin's life in prison had transformed in ways she could never have anticipated. With the training and support of the Irmandade, she has become a formidable fighter and an untouchable presence in the prison's brutal hierarchy.

After two and a half years of gruelling fights, she is no longer just another inmate struggling to survive. She's the undefeated champion of the yard; her reputation is woven into the very fabric of prison life.

The shift happens gradually. It starts with murmurs of her name, whispers by new and seasoned inmates alike. The Brazilian prisoners who don't speak English call her lutadora the fighter, a nickname that spreads quickly. Others who speak English take to calling her the Irish Invincible.

Her victories have become a source of hope for some, fear for others, and fascination for all. No one else has fought with the same intensity and won with such resilience. She's not just respected, she's revered.

Each time she steps into the yard, her presence commands attention. Inmates who used to dismiss her or threaten her, now cheer her name, clapping her on the back or offering respectful nods.

Even the guards take notice, their usual indifference tinged with wariness. They watch her with a mixture of admiration and unease, recognising that Erin has transformed into something they cannot easily control.

But this newfound respect comes with a dark underside. Her reputation has drawn attention not only from fellow inmates and guards but from powers outside the prison walls as well.

One day, after another victorious fight, Erin is approached by a pair of guards with unfamiliar, calculating looks in their eyes. They take her aside, away from the yard, into a quiet, enclosed room she has never seen before.

There, a prison official awaits her, a man whose demeanour is both polished and unsettling.

"Come," one of them says in heavily accented English.

Erin hesitates, her fists still clenched, but the look in their eyes leaves no room for argument. They lead her away from the yard, past the familiar halls of the prison, and through a door she has never noticed before. The air grows cooler as they descend a narrow staircase, the sound of their boots echoing off the concrete walls.

At the bottom of the stairs, they enter a stark, windowless room. A single fluorescent bulb buzzes overhead, casting a harsh light on the man who awaits them.

He is tall and impeccably dressed, his tailored suit a sharp contrast to the grime of the prison. His slicked-back hair and polished demeanour radiate authority. But there is something unsettling about his smile—a coldness that makes Erin's stomach churn.

"Miss O'Connor," he says, his English crisp and deliberate. "I've heard a great deal about you."

Erin says nothing, her muscles tensing as she studies him.

The man gestures for her to sit. When she doesn't move, he chuckles softly and leans against the desk behind him. "I'll get straight to the point. Your skills have caught the attention of someone very powerful. A Saudi monarch, to be precise."

Erin's heart sinks, but she keeps her face expressionless.

"This man," the official continues, "has a keen interest in the underground mixed martial arts circuit. He has offered an extraordinary sum for your…exclusive services."

"What does that mean?" Erin asks, her voice low and steady.

"It means you've been purchased," he replies, the words cutting through the air like a blade. "Your sentence will be pardoned under a special arrangement, but you won't be going free. Instead, you'll be transferred to Saudi Arabia, where you will fight under the monarch's command. For the next 12 years."

Erin feels a surge of anger, but she forces herself to stay calm. "And if I refuse?"

The man's smile faded. "You won't. The alternative is to remain here in this prison, for the rest of your life. A life which—let's be honest—will likely be short and unpleasant."

The guards flanking her, shift slightly, their hands resting on their belts. Erin's gaze flicks to them, noting their rigid stances and the quiet menace in their eyes.

She understands then that the decision has already been made. Refusal wasn't an option.

In the days leading up to her departure, the prison atmosphere shifts subtly around her. Inmates and guards alike treat her with a reverence that borders on awe. She's no longer just the Irish Invincible but a legend. A figure who's risen above the brutal confines of prison life to carve out an identity that no one will forget.

Whispers circulate about her mysterious *release*, rumours spreading like wildfire, though no one knows the full truth.

When the day of her departure arrives, the Irmandade gathers to bid her farewell, their expressions solemn but proud. Rosa embraces her, a rare gesture of affection, and whispers words of encouragement and caution.

The bond they've forged through blood, sweat and survival is unbreakable, even as Erin prepares to leave. Her *family* within these walls has given her the strength to endure, and they send her off with the same fierce spirit that has sustained her throughout her time here.

As she is led out of the prison for the last time, Erin feels a strange mix of emotions—fear, relief, and an aching sense of loss. She steps into the sunlight, blinking against the brightness, and finds herself surrounded by a team of officials, waiting to escort her to a private jet.

This will be her life now: a gilded cage, a world of luxury that masks the underlying control and obligation she will be bound to for the next 12 years.

On the flight to Saudi Arabia, Erin sits quietly, replaying the events of the past two and a half years in her mind. She remembers every fight, every bruise, every brutal lesson she has learned in prison. She thinks of the Irmandade and the fierce bond they share; a connection forged in the darkest moments.

She is no longer the frightened woman who first entered that hellish place; she is something harder, more resilient. And while her future may be bound by chains of a different kind, she knows she possesses a strength that no one can take away from her.

As the plane touches down, Erin steels herself for the new life that awaits. The thought of fighting for someone else's gain, of being a commodity traded for wealth, makes her blood boil, but she keeps her expression calm and resolute.

She will survive this, just as she has survived everything else. The Irish Invincible will endure, and someday, somehow, she will find a way to reclaim her freedom on her own terms.

Erin steps off the plane, her gaze fixed on the horizon: determined and unbroken. Whatever lies ahead, she is ready to face it head-on and will refuse to let anyone—monarch or prison guard—break the spirit she has fought so hard to protect.

Chapter Twelve

Erin's new life in Saudi Arabia unfolds as a surreal blend of freedom and confinement. From the moment she arrives, the stark contrast to her life in Brazil's prison is impossible to ignore. For the first time in years, she is not treated as a number or a nuisance.

Instead, she is treated like an asset—a prized fighter who represents not just her own skill, but the ambitions of the Saudi monarch. Her life becomes a regimented cycle of training, travel and fighting, with every aspect carefully being monitored and orchestrated by her benefactor.

At first, the change is jarring. The stench of sweat, blood and unwashed clothes that defined her existence in Brazil are replaced with clinical cleanliness. Erin is escorted to a private villa within the monarch's sprawling compound.

The villa is modest compared to the opulence of the palace itself but luxurious by any other measure. It has polished marble floors, a bedroom with a large bed that swallowed her in softness, and a private bathroom stocked with scented soaps and fresh towels.

Erin stands in the middle of the room for several minutes, overwhelmed by the sheer unfamiliarity of it all.

Her meals are delivered promptly three times a day and are unlike anything she has eaten in years. Fresh fruits and vegetables, grilled meats, fragrant rice and spiced lentils are laid out on silver trays.

At first, Erin approaches the food cautiously, unsure if it is meant to fatten her up for slaughter or simply show her what she is missing. But as her body adjusts, she realises that this isn't a trick. They want her at her peak—strong, healthy and unbeatable.

Her new wardrobe is another shock to the system. In prison, clothing was limited to ill-fitting uniforms or whatever scraps she could barter for. Now, she is given high-quality athletic wear for training and comfortable, tailored outfits for downtime.

The fabric is soft against her skin, a tactile reminder of how far she has come from the coarse prison uniforms that chafed and tore at her body.

Yet these comforts come with a price. Everything is controlled, from her diet to her training schedule to the precise number of hours she is allowed to rest. Erin quickly learns that her *freedom* is nothing more than an illusion.

Cameras monitor her every move, guards stand at every entrance, and her interactions are limited to a handful of trainers, nutritionists and staff—all of whom treat her with professional courtesy but keep a careful distance.

For all the luxury, Erin knows she is still a prisoner. Her cage is gilded, but it is a cage, nonetheless.

Her fights in Saudi Arabia begin in private arenas and are far removed from the dingy makeshift ring she has grown accustomed to in Brazil. These arenas are pristine and designed to cater to the whims of the wealthy spectators who fill the VIP balconies.

She travels between private arenas in Riyadh and Jeddah and smaller, hidden venues where wealthy spectators gather, eager to watch the notorious *Irish Invincible* in action.

Erin's opponents are formidable skilled fighters, handpicked to challenge her. But she adapts quickly, using every lesson she learned in Brazil to dismantle her adversaries with ruthless precision.

The crowds love her. They cheer her name—The Irish Invincible—in a dozen different accents, their voices echo through the cavernous venues. Erin feels their adoration, their fascination, and she feeds off it.

It reminds her of the prison yard, where every fight was a battle for survival and every victory was a step closer to dominance. But here, the stakes are different. The monarch isn't just gambling on her skill—he is staking his entire reputation.

The stakes aren't just about the fight but about preserving her life outside those walls. She can feel the monarch's watchful gaze in every decision and every fight strategy.

Despite the high stakes, Erin finds herself thriving in this structured environment. She becomes stronger, sharper and more adaptable with each bout. Her experience is making her an indomitable force in the ring.

Within a year, Erin's fame has grown beyond Saudi Arabia. Videos of her fights begin to circulate in underground MMA forums, her name is being whispered among promoters and scouts who see potential in her brutal, unrelenting style.

Offers begin to trickle in from international fight organisers, eager to showcase the infamous *Irish Invincible* in global events.

The idea of entering Erin into the global MMA circuit begins to tantalise him. The monarch sees potential for immense profits and international acclaim, envisioning his name attached to the woman who could, one day, hold championship belts.

Erin's fights in the octagon, under the bright lights of the U.S., mean more than wealth; they can cement her legacy as a prominent figure in the fight world. The monarch wants to see her take on the best; to showcase her skills against opponents worldwide and to bring him recognition and wealth beyond even his current reach.

But it also presents a challenge.

Erin's story is a delicate matter, and the peculiar circumstances of her transfer from Brazil to Saudi Arabia can never come to light.

If word gets out that she has been purchased—that her freedom has been exchanged for a lifetime of servitude—it will raise questions that could tarnish the monarch's carefully curated image. Erin herself is aware of this tightrope, and she walks it with calculated caution.

The first time the possibility of fighting in America is mentioned, Erin feels a flicker of hope she hasn't dared entertain in years. She is summoned to a meeting in the palace complex, her surroundings as intimidating as ever.

The room is adorned with gold accents, the furniture sleek and imposing. The monarch himself is absent, but his officials are there; their expressions are cold and calculating.

They explain the plan: Erin would be entered into the U.S. MMA circuit under a carefully constructed backstory. She would be presented as a mysterious up-and-coming fighter, discovered and trained by the monarch's team. Her victories in Saudi Arabia would serve as her credentials, proof of her skill.

But then comes the warning.

"You will represent His Majesty," one of the officials said, his voice calm but laced with menace. "Every action you take, every word you speak, reflects on him. If you step out of line, if you betray his trust—" He leans forward, his gaze sharp enough to cut. "We will know. And we will find you."

Erin is under no illusion that her life could end swiftly. They have connections everywhere, they assure her—people who can easily reach her, no matter how far she runs.

Erin stares back at the official, her face is unreadable. She has heard threats like this before, but she knows these men aren't bluffing. Their resources, their reach—it is vast and terrifying.

Still, the idea of America plants a seed in her mind. She imagines the crowds, the bright lights of the octagon, and the opportunity to connect with people outside the tightly controlled bubble of her current existence. It isn't freedom, not yet, but it is a step closer. She will bide her time, earn their trust, and find a way to slip through the cracks.

So, Erin eventually politely nods in agreement, meeting their demands with a calm exterior. She knows better than to argue and can imagine the opportunities that could open up in a place like America. She decides that it's a no-brainer and is willing to play the long game. 11 years seems both like an eternity and a countdown.

Her first year in Saudi Arabia has taught her patience and honed her instincts in ways she hadn't anticipated. She has no intention of revealing her reality; she will keep her head down, obey and bide her time.

Each fight would be a step closer to freedom, a step closer to breaking free of this invisible chain. She is a survivor above all else, and she knows that she has the discipline to play this dangerous game, even under watchful eyes.

The weeks leading up to her potential transfer are tense. Erin trains harder than ever, determined to prove that she is ready for the international stage. She pushes her body to its limits: refining her technique, sharpening her reflexes, and studying the styles of fighters she might one day face.

Her trainers notice the change in her, the intensity in her eyes, the fire that burns with every punch and kick. They attribute it to ambition, a hunger for victory, but Erin knows it is something deeper. It is the promise of a life beyond the gilded cage, the possibility of carving out her own destiny.

And so, with the promise of America on the horizon, Erin readies herself. She can taste the possibility of a life beyond this arrangement, and with every ounce of her resolve, she commits to one thing: she will become indispensable, untouchable.

She will rise through the ranks as the Irish Invincible, the fighter who cannot be beaten, and the woman who will fight her way to the top. And when the moment comes—whether it is in the cage or outside of it—she will seize her freedom, one punch, one victory at a time.

The suspense grows with each passing day. Erin is aware that the monarch's decision to send her to America is not yet final. He is weighing the risks, and calculating the rewards, and Erin knows that her every move is being scrutinised. One misstep can shatter the fragile hope she has begun to cling to.

Finally, the call comes. She is to prepare for her very first fight in America, a high-profile bout in Las Vegas that will serve as her debut on the international stage. As she boards the private jet bound for the U.S., Erin feels a mixture of excitement and dread. She is stepping into a new world; one filled with possibilities but fraught with danger.

Erin looks out the jet's window, her reflection is staring back at her. The city lights of Las Vegas glimmer in the distance, a beacon of hope and uncertainty. She clenches her fists, her resolve hardening.

Whatever lies ahead, she will face it head-on. The Irish Invincible isn't just a title—it is her promise to herself. She will survive and thrive, and one day, she will be free.

Chapter Thirteen

Erin's arrival in America marks a stunning shift in her life; one that feels as surreal as it is liberating. After the brutal years spent in a Brazilian prison and the rigid confines of Saudi Arabia, the sprawling penthouse in New York City seems otherworldly.

Floor-to-ceiling windows overlooking Central Park are a living, breathing tapestry of the city's pulse that stretches out beneath her feet. Each night, the glow of the skyline seems to whisper to her: *You're here now. You're closer.*

Her new home is hers, or at least it feels that way. She isn't escorted to and from the property, nor are there any guards shadowing her every step. There are no cameras in the corners of her rooms, and no one monitoring her downtime.

This is a world away from the luxurious but suffocating villa in Saudi Arabia, where her every move was being scrutinised. In America, Erin is given the illusion—and to some extent, the reality—of independence.

For the first time, she can step outside without permission. She can walk through the streets of Manhattan and feel the anonymity of the crowd envelop her, a stark contrast to the watchful eyes that tracked her in Saudi Arabia.

She isn't truly free—her agreement with the Saudis still looms over her—but she has room to breathe, to think, and to reclaim pieces of herself that have been buried under years of survival.

Her new life comes with resources she can hardly believe. The team assembling around her are world-class, and their sole purpose is to make her the best fighter she can be. Her trainers push her harder than anyone ever has before, but their methods are precise and scientific.

They tailor every aspect of her regimen to her needs, from high-altitude training to cutting-edge recovery techniques.

Her nutritionist, a sharp-tongued woman named Diana, fusses over Erin's meals with the care of a mother hen; ensuring every bite is perfectly balanced to fuel her body. Erin's medic, Dr Reese, monitors her health with military precision, always watching for the first signs of strain or injury.

Even her trainers, as intense as they are, bring a warmth and camaraderie to their work that Erin has never encountered before. For a while, their kindness unsettles her—it feels too foreign, too fragile.

Slowly, though, she allows herself to relax, just a little. She laughs at Diana's grumbling over her refusal to eat kale and endures Dr Reese's relentless lectures about hydration with a quiet smirk.

These small interactions become part of a rhythm that feels dangerously close to normalcy, though Erin keeps her emotional distance. She cannot afford to form real connections.

Her solitude remains her sanctuary. The walls of the penthouse become her refuge. When she isn't training or fighting, she sits by the window for hours, staring out at the sprawling city below.

New York has a way of making her feel both small and powerful at the same time. It reminds her of Dublin, but bigger, louder, with an unrelenting energy that pulls her forward.

For the sake of marketing, the team around her refines Erin's image. The scars that map her skin—remnants of her brutal past—are minimised where possible. They are either softened with carefully placed tattoos or concealed through surgical procedures.

But they don't erase all of them; a few scars are left untouched, allowed to remain visible to evoke fear in her opponents and hint at the intensity of her journey. Each one tells part of her story, giving her an intimidating, almost mythic aura that heightens the spectacle of her fights.

The significance of her GAA jersey emerges as a defining symbol of Erin's journey. It isn't just an aesthetic choice or a marketing ploy—it is deeply personal.

The jersey was a gift from Callum, her closest friend during her summer in the Gaeltacht in Donegal, back when she was 15 and full of dreams. Callum had been her anchor that summer. A kind, steady presence during a time when she'd felt untethered.

The jersey itself was from Callum's own county team, and he had given it to her on her last day in the Gaeltacht, a gesture she hadn't fully understood at the time.

"This is for you, in case you ever forget where you come from," he'd said, pressing it into her hands.

Erin had laughed then, thinking he was being dramatic, but she'd kept the jersey, nonetheless.

Years later, in Saudi Arabia, and now America, that jersey has become a talisman. It is one of the few possessions she has managed to hold onto during her darkest days, a thread connecting her to a version of herself that felt like a distant memory. Now, as the Irish Invincible, she wears it into the octagon, not just as a nod to her Irish roots but as a symbol of defiance.

The jersey represents the fighting spirit of GAA players—athletes who play, not for money or fame, but for the pride of their communities—giving every ounce of their strength. They're warriors, playing out of pure loyalty and love for their roots.

It is a reminder that, like them, she is fighting for something bigger than herself. For Erin, every time she steps into the cage wearing that jersey, she feels a surge of purpose. It isn't just about survival anymore; it is about reclaiming her story—piece by piece.

The first time she enters the Octagon in America, wearing the jersey, the reaction is electric. The lights dim, the arena roars, and Erin strides into the cage with the calm confidence of a seasoned warrior. The jersey—green and white with bold Gaelic lettering—stands out starkly against her scarred skin.

The fans are captivated. Here is this fierce, Irish fighter, walking into the ring like a Gaelic warrior stepping onto a battlefield. Her image resonates deeply, particularly with Irish Americans and the Irish diaspora.

They see in her, a reflection of their own struggles, their own stories of resilience. Erin becomes a sensation almost overnight; her fan base is swelling with every victory.

Her fights are more than competitions—they are spectacles. The scars that haven't been concealed tell a story of survival and strength, adding to her mythos. Audiences speculate about her past, filling in the blanks with their own imaginations. To them, she isn't just a fighter; she is a symbol of unbreakable spirit.

Despite her growing fame, Erin never loses sight of her reality. The Saudis still hold her leash, and she knows the cost of stepping out of line.

Her penthouse, her trainers, even her freedom to walk the streets—they are all part of a carefully constructed illusion. But Erin is playing the long game. Every fight and every cheer from the crowd brings her closer to her goal.

She wears the jersey as her armour, a silent reminder of where she comes from and what she is fighting for. It is her link to Callum, to Ireland, and to the girl she used to be before the world stripped her bare. And it is a quiet act of rebellion against the forces that seek to control her.

With each victory, Erin's reputation grows, and so does the legend of the Irish Invincible. As she knocks down opponent after opponent, the tales of her ferocity, skill and indomitable spirit, spread across the MMA circuit. Her name begins to echo in gyms, arenas and sports bars across the country.

Yet, behind her stoic expression, Erin knows her journey is far from over. She remains ever aware of the silent contract hanging over her, of the years she must endure in the cage until her time is finally her own. For now, though, she has one thing she has never had before: the hope that each fight, each roar of the crowd, brings her one step closer to breaking free.

America, this new stage in her life, is an opportunity, a stepping stone towards a future she still dares to dream about. She will continue to don the jersey, to stand tall as the Irish

Invincible, all the while keeping her eye on the ultimate goal—freedom.

And until that day comes, she fights, with every ounce of strength and every scar she has earned along the way.

Chapter Fourteen

Erin sits alone in the dim light of her penthouse, flexing her fingers against the familiar ache in her knuckles. The pain is a constant companion now, a sharp reminder of nine years of brutal battles.

She looks down at her hands, the skin rough and uneven, and her knuckles are thickening from countless breaks and fractures. Each fight has taken a piece of her, and the strain is etched deep into her body.

Her knees creak when she stands, and her joints are stiff from years of relentless training and impact. The sharp twinge in her right shoulder—a lingering injury from a fight three years earlier—reminds her of the toll the octagon has taken.

She is still fierce, still undefeated, but the truth is undeniable: her body is wearing down. Even the best recovery methods, the meticulous diet, and the elite medical care can't stop time.

At 35, Erin is no longer the unstoppable force she had been in her 20s. Her opponents are younger, their bodies fresh and unbroken by years of combat. They move faster, hit harder and recover quicker. Every fight requires more effort to prepare and more grit to endure.

Yet she has persevered, fuelled by sheer willpower and the knowledge that every victory brings her closer to freedom. But now, as the end of her contract looms on the horizon, she is facing a decision she has been avoiding for months: she can't keep fighting until her body gives up completely.

Erin has always been a fighter, but she doesn't want to end her career being dragged out of the cage. She wants to leave on her own terms—undefeated—a champion who has never been broken.

She has fought her way through the darkest of circumstances and survived. Now, she wants to finish as the fighter who has endured it all and stands unshaken.

The meeting with the Saudis is set for a week's time. Erin prepares for it the way she prepares for a fight: with precision and determination. This is her chance to walk away with dignity, and she isn't going to let it slip through her fingers.

The room they brought her to, is as opulent as ever, with artistic walls and marble floors. But Erin no longer feels awed or intimidated.

She has spent almost a decade under their control and is no longer the desperate woman they had plucked from a Brazilian prison. She has built a legacy, a name that transcended borders. She is the Irish Invincible, and she knows her worth.

The Saudis enter the room in silence, their expressions are unreadable. These are the men who have turned her into a commodity, an asset that has made them fortunes beyond their wildest dreams.

Her undefeated streak has become a cornerstone of their empire, her image is plastered on posters, action figures and apparel, selling to fans around the globe. They know as well as she does that Erin isn't just a fighter—she is a brand.

Erin stands while they sit, meeting their gazes without flinching. "I need to retire," she says, her voice steady and calm. "Nine years of this—my body's at its breaking point. My hands are ruined, my joints are deteriorating, and every fight takes longer to recover from.

"I can't keep doing this, not at the level you expect. And you know as well as I do, that the moment I lose, my value drops."

The Saudis exchange glances but say nothing, so Erin presses on, "I've given you my all, and I've kept my end of the deal. I'm undefeated, and I've built a legacy that will sell for years. But if I keep fighting, that streak is going to end.

"And when it does, you lose the myth—the legend. You don't want me limping out of the cage after a loss—you want me walking away at the top, untouchable."

Her words hang in the air, heavy with truth. The Saudis lean back in their chairs, their expressions thoughtful. Erin can see the calculations running through their minds, the way they weigh her arguments against their plans.

One of the men, an older official with sharp eyes, finally speaks. "You've built something remarkable," he says slowly. "The undefeated streak, the name—it's all part of what makes you valuable. Retiring now *would* mean we can continue to sell that image, that story, for decades.

"Merchandise, documentaries, appearances—it's true that the undefeated champion has more value than the ageing fighter. It's clear that you have thought this through."

Another man nods, his fingers tapping against the table. "The timing is important. If you were to lose, the mystique would be gone. But if you leave now, undefeated, the legend remains intact."

Erin stays silent, letting them work through the logic she has presented. She can see the shift in their expressions as they come to terms with the decision.

They always anticipated wringing every last fight out of her, but they couldn't ignore the financial sense in her argument. Erin's legacy as an undefeated champion is worth more than a few more matches.

After what feels like an eternity, the older official speaks again. "We agree," he says, his tone brisk. "You will retire immediately. Your contract will be terminated, and you will be free to leave. Your legacy will remain as it is—untouched, undefeated."

Relief washes over Erin, but she keeps her expression composed. She has won this fight, the most important one so far in her life and she isn't about to let them see her falter. She stands up, nods her appreciation, and leaves the room without looking back.

The first time Erin steps out into the world without the weight of her contract, it doesn't feel real. She walks the streets of Manhattan, blending into the crowd. She is no longer a fighter bound by agreements and obligations. She is free to choose her own path, her own future.

The pain in her hands, her knees, her shoulder—it is still there, but it feels lighter now. These scars and aches are reminders of everything she has endured to reach this moment. She is tired, yes, but she is also undefeated. She has fought for nine gruelling years and has come out the other side with her legacy intact.

Erin's name will live on in the world of MMA, her story will be told and retold by fans and media alike. Posters, action figures, and apparel will continue to sell, the image of the Irish Invincible remaining as iconic as ever. But Erin isn't thinking about any of that.

Now, for the first time, Erin can envision a life of her own, one where she is not bound by contracts or driven by survival, where every day is her choice.

As she steps away from the only life she has known for so many years, she carries with her not only the scars but the knowledge of what she has survived and the strength that brought her through it all.

For the first time in nearly a decade, Erin has no one telling her where to go, what to do, or how to live. As she wanders through the streets of Manhattan, a strange feeling settles over her—freedom. It is exhilarating but also unfamiliar, almost disorienting. For years, her life had been dictated by others.

First by Fabio, then prisoners and prison guards in Brazil, and then by the Saudis, who orchestrated every aspect of her existence. Now, it is all up to her, and the weight of that reality hit her with equal parts relief and uncertainty. She imagines what her life will be like—now.

No more punishing training schedules. No more stepping into the octagon, bracing for the pain and brutality of a fight. She can do anything she ever wanted—if only she can figure out what that was.

Erin tried to remember the things she used to dream about before her life had been turned upside down; back when she was just a girl from Tyrone. She was full of fire and ambition.

She thought about the open landscapes of Ireland, the rolling hills she hadn't seen in years.

She imagined walking along a beach in Donegal, the cold Atlantic wind whipping her hair as she breathed in the salty air. She imagined sitting in a cosy pub, the sound of traditional music filling the room, a pint of Guinness in her hand. For so long, these had been distant fantasies, glimpses of a world she thought she might never see again.

Now, they were within her reach. But as the possibilities unfurled before her, so did the shadows of her past. Erin thought about her family—her mother, father and extended relations. She hasn't heard a word from them in all the years she has been in America. Surely, they know about her.

She was the Irish Invincible, a name plastered across sports headlines, a figure revered and feared in the MMA world. How could they not have seen her fights, her interviews, her face on posters and magazine covers? The thought fills her with profound sadness.

She imagines, at first, that they might have been ashamed of her, of the choices that had led her to prison. But as her fame grew, she wonders if shame could truly explain their silence. Had they disowned her entirely?

Or had they decided that the woman they saw in the cage—the scarred, ferocious fighter—was no longer the daughter they had known?

Erin thought of her mother, who always tried to keep the family close, even when they struggled to make ends meet. She thinks of her father; a quiet man who had taught her to stand her ground and fight for what mattered.

Did they still think like that? Or had they turned away from her, unwilling to reconcile the person she had become with the person she used to be? The idea of returning to Ireland is both comforting and terrifying. She longed to see the familiar streets of her hometown, to reconnect with the people who shaped her.

But what if they didn't want to see her? What if she had been gone too long, and the person she had become was a stranger to them now? Erin wrestled with these thoughts as she walks through Central Park, the crisp winter air stinging her cheeks.

Freedom is a gift, but it comes with its own challenges. For years, she has focused only on survival, on winning the next fight, and on fulfilling her contract, so she could, one day be free. Now that the fight is over, she is left with questions she doesn't know how to answer.

She tries to picture herself showing up unannounced at her parents' home, knocking on the door after all these years. Would they greet her with open arms? Or would they turn her away? She imagines, sitting at the kitchen table, sharing a meal with her family; the way they used to before everything had fallen apart.

But she also imagines the awkward silences, the unspoken questions, that will be the painful reminders of all the years she has lost. Erin has always been strong, but the thought of facing her family again makes her feel vulnerable in a way she hadn't felt in years. The octagon is brutal, but it is a brutality she understands.

The wounds she endured there were physical, and they healed in time. The wounds of rejection, of loss—those were harder to face. Still, she couldn't shake the idea of going home. It lingers in the back of her mind—a faint hope that maybe, just maybe—she can rebuild some of what she has lost.

She isn't sure if she is ready to take that step yet, but the thought gave her something to hold on to—a purpose beyond fighting, beyond survival. For now, Erin is focused on putting one foot in front of the other. She will take her time and figure out what she wants her life to be.

But as she walks through the streets of Manhattan, surrounded by the noise and energy of the city, she carries with her the quiet hope of one day finding her way back to the people and the place's that shaped her earlier years.

It is a hope she isn't ready to let go of, even if it means facing the pain of her past.

Chapter Fifteen

It is a monumental day for Erin when she is handed her passport. It feels strange in her hands, almost foreign, after all these years of life dictated by others. Along with it, the Saudis present her with a modest stack of cash—just enough to cover six months' rent in Dublin City if she lives frugally.

The amount is a stark reminder of how little she has left from the fortune she generated for others, and it's hard not to feel a pang of resentment. Still, Erin doesn't linger on it. Freedom is worth more than all the money in the world, and at last, she has it.

As she boards the plane in New York, there's an electric excitement pulsing through her, the kind of thrill she had forgotten. She's heading back to Dublin; back to the city where her life had taken so many turns, and where, for the first time, she can live life on her own terms.

She imagines what her future might look like—exploring the city again, finding new work, and maybe, just maybe, discovering a real sense of peace.

Yet, as the flight progresses, those feelings of excitement start to fade. In their place, comes a growing sense of nervousness, the same queasy sensation she felt years ago on that first bus trip from Tyrone to Dublin.

Back then, she'd been a young woman setting off for her first taste of independence, though naive and uncertain of what lay ahead. This time, she's older, stronger and shaped by experiences that have left indelible marks on her—both visible and invisible. But somehow, that sense of dread is just as sharp, just as real.

The more she thinks about it, the more she realises how much has changed. Her life with Fabio was all she ever knew of Dublin, and without him, the city feels like uncharted territory again. She'll be starting from scratch in a place that used to feel familiar but now will feel eerily distant.

Her heart begins to pound at the thought of facing Dublin alone, with only her own resilience to lean on. It's not the city she fears, but the daunting challenge of building a life without any of the people or structures she once relied on.

Returning to Tyrone isn't an option, and she feels a familiar bitterness at the thought of the people she left behind. Family and friends—they'd all faded from her life as they were too uncomfortable with her choices; too quick to judge or turn away when she needed them most.

Time has dulled the sharpness of her resentment, but now, thinking of the isolation that lies ahead, those feelings start to resurface. There's no homecoming in Tyrone for her, no warm welcome waiting with open arms.

As the plane descends over Dublin, Erin steels herself. She reminds herself of everything she has endured—the violence, the manipulation, the years of struggle. She has survived it all, and she's determined to build a life on her own terms, whatever that may look like.

Maybe she won't have the support of family or a partner, but for the first time, she has her freedom. And that's more than she could have dreamed of when she first left Tyrone all those years ago. By the time the wheels touch down in Dublin, Erin feels a flicker of resolve. Whatever awaits her now, she's ready to face it head-on, alone if necessary.

She steps off the plane into a city that is both familiar and unknown. As she takes her first steps into her new life, she promises herself that this time, she'll make her own choices, and carve her own path, without letting anyone else control her fate.

Erin's return to Dublin has been nothing like she had imagined. In her mind, coming home is supposed to feel like reclaiming a piece of herself, a way to close the gap between the girl she'd once been and the woman she'd become.

Instead, it feels like starting over in a city she barely recognises. It is not the Dublin she had left behind, and she is not the Erin, who, once roamed its streets with dreams too big for her own good.

Her first task is finding a place to live, but even that proves more difficult than expected. She has spent years living under someone else's control—in the confines of prison and the brutal monotony of training camps. Also, in the luxurious penthouse that had been as much a prison as any cage.

She wants something simple now. A place that is hers and hers alone, where she won't have to answer to anyone.

But Dublin has changed since she last called it home. Rents are astronomical, and the search for a one-bedroom flat quickly became a sobering reality check.

Erin has a modest sum saved from her years in America—not as much as people might imagine, given her fame, but enough to give her a start. Even so, she baulks at the prices she sees for tiny, run-down apartments with peeling paint and questionable plumbing.

The idea of sharing a flat with strangers is out of the question. She can't imagine living with anyone, having to explain her scars, her silences, and her unwillingness to connect. She needs privacy; a place where she can shut out the world.

So, she keeps searching, walking through neighbourhoods—that once felt familiar but now seem alien—scrolling through listings late into the night. Her frustration is mounting with each passing day.

Eventually, she finds a one-bedroom in a nondescript block on the outskirts of the city. It isn't much to look at—just a small, boxy flat with beige walls and cheap laminate floors—but it is clean and quiet.

The building itself is uninspired, with a drab grey structure with little character, and her view is of a car park rather than anything scenic. Still, it is hers, and that's what matters the most.

The rent is higher than she wants to pay, but she doesn't have the energy to keep looking. She signs the lease and moves in with nothing but a duffel bag and the ghost of a hope that this might be the start of something better.

Settling into the flat is another matter entirely. Erin buys only the basics—a bed, a small table and a chair. She doesn't bother decorating. She tells herself it is because she doesn't care.

But deep down, she knows it is because she isn't sure how long she will stay. The flat feels like a liminal space, not a home but a place to hide while she figures out her next move.

At first, the solitude is a relief. She had been surrounded by people for so long—trainers, managers, medics and promoters—all of them watching her, controlling her and managing her.

Here, there is no one to answer to. She can sleep in, if she wants, eat what she likes, and spend her days however she chooses. But as the days stretch into weeks, that freedom begins to feel like a weight.

Boredom becomes her constant companion. She has no job, no routine and no one to talk to. She wanders the city aimlessly, her scarf pulled up high and her hat pulled low to avoid recognition.

She avoids the areas that remind her too much of her old life, but even so, memories creep in unbidden. Every corner seems to whisper a fragment of the past, and the more she tries to push it away, the more it seems to cling to her.

It is during this void of boredom and isolation that her thoughts begin to drift towards Fabio. She hasn't thought of him in years, or so she tells herself. But back in Dublin, his memory comes flooding back with an intensity that surprises her.

She remembers the way he laughed; the way he'd make her feel invincible before the world taught her what that word truly meant. She remembers the wild nights they'd spent together and the fire that burned between them before everything fell apart.

And she remembers the way it had ended—the betrayal, the heartbreak, the realisation that the love she thought they'd shared had been a lie.

Fabio had been her first great mistake; a lesson learned the hard way. She knows that. And yet, here she is, sitting alone in her drab little flat, thinking about him. The rational part of her screams at her to let it go, to leave the past where it belonged.

But the loneliness, the boredom, the gnawing sense of emptiness—they all conspire to make her wonder, just for a moment, what it would be like to see him again.

She imagines finding him, walking into some pub or café and locking eyes with the man who once set her world on fire. Would he recognise her? Would he care?

The thought is absurd, and she hates herself for even entertaining it. Fabio is a ghost from another life, a reminder of the girl she used to be. She isn't that girl anymore, and she doesn't want to be.

And yet, the idea lingers. It isn't about love—not really. Erin knows better than to think Fabio could give her anything she needs. It is about the pull of the familiar, the desperate need for connection in a city that suddenly feels so alien.

She knows it is dangerous, even foolish to let herself think this way. She tells herself she will not act on it, and that it is just a passing thought born of boredom and isolation.

But the thought won't leave her, and as the days pass, it begins to fester like a wound she can't quite heal. Erin doesn't know what scares her more—that she might actually try to find him, or that she might not, and be left alone with nothing but her memories and her regrets.

For now, she does nothing, letting the idea sit in the back of her mind like a secret she can't admit even to herself.

Chapter Sixteen

Erin has always been resourceful—sometimes, to her detriment. When the idea of finding Fabio first takes hold of her, she tries to brush it off, reasoning that there is no sense in reopening old wounds that are barely scarred over. But the more she resists, the stronger the pull becomes.

It begins as a fleeting thought, an almost laughable notion she immediately dismisses, telling herself she's stronger now, smarter. But the thought takes root, persistent and relentless, until it becomes a whisper in the back of her mind; growing louder with each passing day.

She tells herself it's curiosity, a way to face her past. But deep down, she knows it's more complicated than that. She feels the pull towards him like a phantom limb; a connection she doesn't want but cannot sever.

The idea of seeing him—even from a distance—feels like a small thread she can grasp onto, something tangible in the vast, shapeless fog of her current existence. Yet, even as she reaches for it, she knows it's a thread that could unravel everything she's built.

Her logical mind warns her against it. She knows better than to reach out directly—too risky and foolish. The thought of him knowing she's back fills her with dread, but not as much as the idea of seeing him fills her with longing. She has worked so hard to rebuild her life, to create something whole from the broken pieces he left behind.

She knows better than anyone how dangerous it is to revisit the past, and how fragile the foundation of her new life really is. But there's an emptiness inside her she can't ignore, a gnawing void that she has tried to fill. But nothing has silenced the echoes of him: of who she was before him, or what she has lost.

The urge to find Fabio becomes a distraction, a lifeline she clings to in the storm of her uncertainty. It starts innocently enough: small, tentative steps, like searching social media profiles and scanning old connections for clues.

Each step feels like a betrayal of her hard-won progress, but she justifies it by telling herself she's only looking; only trying to understand where he is, or who he is now. She frames it as closure, a final act of facing the thing she's avoided for years.

But the truth is more complicated, tangling in layers of fear, regret and a deep, unspoken hope that she doesn't dare name. As the days pass, her search becomes an obsession. She finds herself watching, waiting and combing through old memories like a detective piecing together a case.

Her heart feels heavy with the weight of it, each revelation about his life now—a job, a neighbourhood, a routine—pulling her further into the past.

She still tells herself it isn't about wanting him back—God, no. It is about closure. About finally facing the person who has shaped so much of her pain, who still haunts her thoughts even when she wants nothing more than to forget him.

At first, she hesitates to look for him directly, fearing it will make her complicit in reigniting a connection she isn't prepared to handle. But slowly, methodically, she begins piecing together clues. It isn't difficult to find traces of him—Fabio had always been the type to leave a trail.

Social media, friends of friends, and casual conversations she initiates under the guise of curiosity. His life hasn't gone completely under the radar; there are snippets to be found if one knows where to look. She discovers that he is still in Dublin, which doesn't surprise her.

He'd always had a fondness for the city's chaos and charm. But beyond that, details are harder to pin down. He isn't particularly active online, and when he is, he leaves breadcrumbs that lead nowhere—a tagged photo here, a mention there.

It is enough to frustrate her, to keep her awake at night, but not enough to give her what she needs. So, Erin decides to rely on what she knows about him, and the things she remembers from before her life with him shattered. Fabio always loved coffee bars, particularly those, open late at night.

He'd called them his *thinking spots*. Places where he could lounge in dim light with a book, a notepad, or simply his thoughts. She can still picture him sitting by a fogged-up window, his hands wrapped around a mug, his dark eyes scanning the room like he owned it.

Back then, she'd loved that about him—the quiet confidence, the way he seemed to inhabit every space as if it were made for him. Now, the memory felt like a weight pressing on her chest. Erin maps out the city in her mind, remembering the places he would frequent.

She starts with his old haunts: the small, tucked-away cafes where he'd charmed her into countless late-night conversations. But many of those places are gone now. They are replaced by new businesses or swallowed by Dublin's ever-changing streetscape.

The ones that remain are devoid of him—nothing but empty chairs and strangers sipping their lattes. Undeterred, she expands her search. She begins visiting newer, trendier spots; the kind of places she thinks Fabio would like.

He always had a knack for finding places with just the right atmosphere: a balance of intimacy and vibrancy, a touch of edge but not pretension. It isn't hard for her to imagine where he might go now, even after all these years. Weeks pass like this.

Her life becomes a blur of late-night stakeouts, coffee cups draining to the dregs, and hours spent scanning faces in the glow of warm café lights. It is exhausting and exhilarating. A strange mix of dread and anticipation that keeps her going, even when she knows she should stop.

She tells herself that she is being ridiculous and that this is a dangerous game to play. But the truth is, she doesn't actually know how to stop. And then, one cold January evening, it happens. Erin has almost decided to give up for the night.

The café she has been sitting in—a cosy but modern spot tucked into a quiet street corner—is beginning to thin out, its patrons drifting away into the night. She has been nursing a cup of tea for the better part of an hour, her nerves raw from too many nights like this.

As she stands to leave, something makes her pause—a familiar figure stepping through the door. It's him. It's Fabio.

Her breath catches in her throat as she takes him in. He looks older, of course. His hair has thinned slightly, and there are lines around his eyes she doesn't remember from before.

But it is unmistakably him. That same strong jawline, the same broad shoulders, the same casual ease with which he moves, as though the world bends to accommodate him. He scans the room as he walks in, his gaze passing over her without recognition. For a moment, she freezes.

Time seems to slow as memories come rushing back: the first time she'd been with him in a place just like this; the way he'd smiled at her as if he already knew the ending to their story. And then, the darker memories—the ones she tried so hard to forget—push their way to the surface.

The accusations, the gaslighting, the fear that settles like a permanent shadow over her life. Fabio orders his coffee and finds a seat by the window. Erin stays rooted to the spot, her heart pounding in her chest. She can't believe it—after weeks of searching, she has finally found him.

And now that she has, she doesn't know what to do. Part of her wants to turn and run, to put as much distance between them as possible and never look back. But another part of her—the part that has driven her to find him in the first place—keeps her there, watching him from the safety of the shadows.

She tells herself she isn't ready to leave yet. Not until she knows what kind of man he is now. Fabio, wow. For a moment, it feels like the air has been knocked from her lungs. He's older now, well into his 40s, but he hasn't changed much. There's still that rugged handsomeness, that easy confidence in his stride that once captivated her.

At that moment, she feels the old pull towards him rising up; a rush of feelings she thought she'd buried. It's almost cruel how easily her body remembers. Her heart is stirring in ways that make her feel foolish and weak. But the spell breaks as quickly as it begins.

A flood of memories comes crashing through her, tearing through the thin veneer of her longing. She remembers the charm that had once drawn her in, only to become the weapon he used to keep her under his control.

She remembers the isolation, the manipulation, and the constant accusations that wore her down until she questioned her own reality.

And she remembers the end of it all—the night when his cruelty boiled over into something she could no longer endure. The night she finally escaped from his clutches, although it felt like she left a part of herself behind with the consequences that followed.

Now, seeing him here, so casual and carefree, feels like a cruel mockery of everything she has endured. How can he look so normal, and so untouched by the chaos he caused?

Hatred surges in her chest, hot and consuming. How dare he go about his life as if nothing happened? How dare he exist in the same world, walking the same streets, and breathing the same air as her, after all he did to destroy her? For a fleeting, burning moment, she wants to confront him.

She wants to march up to him and demand answers, to make him see her, and to force him to acknowledge the pain he caused. But she knows better. Confronting Fabio now will be a disaster; a reckless act that could shatter the careful walls she's built around herself.

It won't give her the closure she craves; it will only drag her back into his orbit, a place she's worked so hard to escape. Instead, Erin forces herself to stay calm. She watches him from a distance with her heart pounding in her chest, and her hands trembling at her sides.

She tells herself she needs to be smart about this. She needs to see who he is now, to know if he's changed. Or, if he's still the man who manipulated and controlled her. And deep down, there's a part of her that feels responsible—a part of her that needs to know if he has left a trail of other women like her; each of them a victim of his charm and cruelty.

The thought of him hurting someone else ignites something protective in her, a fierce determination that pushes aside her fear. She knows this is a bad idea, and she's playing with fire. But she can't help herself. She has come too far to turn back now.

And so, she stays. She watches. She waits. And with every passing moment, the knot in her chest tightens, because she knows that this isn't just about him. It's about her—about the version of herself she lost and the part of her that's still searching for a way.

Chapter Seventeen

When Fabio leaves the café, Erin cannot resist her urges any longer and she decides to follow him. She hangs back, keeping her distance, watching him from the shadows as he exits the coffee shop and makes his way through the streets of Dublin.

She feels a strange sense of power, shadowing him the way he once was shadowing her mind; controlling the situation in a way she hadn't been able to all those years ago. This time, she's the one in control, choosing how and when to make herself known.

Fabio, oblivious, continues his day, weaving his way through familiar neighbourhoods, exchanging pleasantries with people here and there. He laughs easily and even stops to chat with a woman who seems charmed by him. Erin watches, feeling anger twist in her gut.

How easily he can still captivate people, she thinks bitterly.

How effortlessly he can wear the mask of a kind, charming man when she knows all too well what lurks beneath. Watching him interact with others fills her with both anger and a strange sense of purpose. She wants to see more and understand if this really is an act or if some part of him has genuinely changed.

For hours, she trails him, studying his behaviour and his interactions. She notices how he seems to gravitate towards women, always with that magnetic charm, his gestures open, his smile disarming.

But Erin knows the truth beneath it all, and with each passing minute, her hatred grows, tempers by a chilling resolve. She wonders how many people he has hurt. How many others have fallen victim to his charms? She's here now to witness him, to understand him and, maybe—just maybe—to put an end to his cycle of harm.

Erin's shadowing of Fabio grows more intense as she pieces together the details of his life. Each day, she learns a little more about the man who once held her world in his grip. After trailing him from one stop to the next, she finally discovers where Fabio lives, it feels like both a victory and a shameful defeat.

The sleek, modern apartment complex is a far cry from the modest place they'd shared during their time together. Its polished exterior, the well-dressed residents coming and going, the quiet hum of luxury—it all screams success. Standing across the street in the rain, Erin feels a complicated rush of emotions.

She's furious that he has done so well for himself. He appears to have escaped their shared past unscathed, while she has spent years clawing her way back from the wreckage.

But there's also a part of her that feels vindicated like she has regained a sliver of power simply by knowing where he lays his head at night.

Not only that, but she soon finds out that he owns a high-end gym not far from the city centre. It is frequented by a mix of fitness enthusiasts, professionals and athletes.

Fabio has, it seems, done well for himself. The gym is spacious and impeccably designed with state-of-the-art equipment, and a dedicated staff that clearly respects him.

She watches him there, moving among the members with that familiar charisma, offering training tips, shaking hands and laughing with clients. Everyone seems to like him and even admire him.

Erin sees him through the tinted windows, conducting himself as the approachable yet authoritative figure she once thought he was back when she first fell for him.

She begins to wonder if this new life has indeed shaped him into a different man—a man who no longer feels the need to control or hurt the people around him.

Then, she notices someone else, a woman who enters the gym and is greeted warmly by Fabio. She's beautiful, with a sunny smile and a kindness in her eyes that instantly reminds Erin of her younger self. Through her careful observations, Erin realises that this woman, Gemma, is Fabio's girlfriend.

At a guess, she's not far from 30—youthful and lively, just as Erin was when she first stepped off the bus from Tyrone. As Erin watches the two of them together, her mind spins with conflicted feelings. There's an ache in her chest; a strange mixture of envy and protectiveness.

Gemma seems to bring out something soft in Fabio, a gentleness Erin doesn't remember him ever having with her. He appears attentive and caring, taking her hand as they chat and exchanging quiet smiles.

For a fleeting moment, Erin feels a pang of hope.

Maybe he has changed.

The thought is disorienting, filling her with a dizzying mix of anger, relief and confusion. Is it possible that time has shaped him into a better man? Had he genuinely outgrown the violent controlling streak that once defined their relationship?

She can't shake the possibility, and it unsettles her. After all, he's surrounded by people who seem to like him, even respect him. He has built a successful business and established a life that doesn't look like it holds the darkness she remembers.

But Erin's instincts caution her against letting her guard down. She knows better than anyone how expertly Fabio can wear the mask of a good man. There is always that charm, that allure, which he projects so effortlessly.

Yet, beneath it had been a storm of manipulation and cruelty that only those closest to him ever truly saw. She wonders if Gemma has any idea of what might lurk under the surface—or if, like Erin once did, she sees only what Fabio wants her to see.

Despite her uncertainty, Erin decides she needs more time to observe. She won't let herself be fooled by his outward appearance, or by the life he has managed to build. So, she follows him for several more days: studying his every move, watching his interactions, and waiting for any sign of the man she knew all too well.

She watches him with Gemma, waiting for a flash of anger, a subtle tightening of his grip on her arm, an expression that hints at something darker. She wants to believe he has changed, for Gemma's sake as much as her own. But if he hasn't—if he's still the same man underneath—then she knows that she'll have to act.

Each day, Erin's conviction wavers between hope and doubt. She's determined to uncover the truth, no matter how painful it might be, and make sure that this time, Fabio cannot hurt anyone the way he once hurt her.

Erin's resolve to follow Fabio quickly becomes an all-encompassing obsession, though she doesn't recognise it as such. To her, this is a necessary act and a way of confronting her past without diving headfirst into its darkness. But the truth is more insidious.

What begins as a need to see him from a distance, spirals into a fixation she can't shake. Each morning, she wakes with a singular purpose: to know more and to uncover the truth about who Fabio is now. Her days are no longer her own. They revolve entirely around him. The tracking starts small.

She lingers outside his gym, watching him through tinted windows as he moves through his day. She notes his routines, the hours he arrives and departs, and the way he interacts with his staff and clients.

But soon, her curiosity deepens, and she finds herself mapping out the places he frequents, trying to anticipate his movements. She spends hours walking the streets of Dublin, retracing his steps from the day before, hoping to catch glimpses of him and piece together the puzzle of his life.

Her phone becomes a tool of obsession. She jots down notes in the margins of her planner. It is a growing list of locations, times and interactions. She scours social media for clues about his personal life, even creating a fake profile to follow the gym's Instagram page.

Each new discovery feels like progress, a step closer to understanding the man who once controlled every aspect of her world. But with each step, Erin unknowingly slips further into a pattern of behaviour she swore she would never entertain.

She tells herself that she's being logical and pragmatic. She convinces herself that this isn't stalking—it's research. Observation. Preparation. After all, she has no intention of speaking to Fabio, no plan to confront him. She's simply gathering information, arming herself with the truth.

But deep down, in the quiet corners of her mind, she knows there's more to it than that. She doesn't want to admit that she feels a strange thrill each time she spots him; a mix of dread and satisfaction that keeps her coming back. That night, she dreams of him.

In her dream, he's the man she first fell for—charming, attentive, the man who swept her off her feet and promised her the world. But as dreams do, it shifts suddenly, and she finds herself trapped in their old apartment, with the walls closing in.

Fabio's voice is echoing around her as he demands to know where she has been; who she has spoken to; what she has done.

She wakes in a cold sweat, her heart pounding, the edges of the dream clinging to her like cobwebs. Despite the dream's warning, Erin doesn't slow down. If anything, she doubles her efforts. She begins following Fabio more closely, shadowing him as he moves through his days.

She hangs back, careful to keep her distance, but the act of following him becomes second nature. Each step feels calculated and controlled. For the first time in years, she feels like she holds the upper hand.

Erin turns her thoughts on Gemma. When Erin noticed Gemma for the first time, something inside her shifted.

She thinks back on when Fabio greeted the young woman with warmth and affection, and how that stirred a storm of emotions that Erin wasn't prepared for. At first, it's anger—a hot, seething rage that he could so easily move on, with someone unburdened by the past.

But beneath the anger is something else, something more vulnerable. A pang of protectiveness. Erin continues to study Gemma from afar, observing the way she carries herself, and the way she looks at Fabio with a mixture of admiration and trust. It's so familiar it makes Erin's stomach turn.

Gemma still reminds her too much of herself—young, hopeful, unaware of what lurks beneath Fabio's polished exterior. Erin's anger gives way to a chilling determination. She has to protect Gemma. She can't let another woman fall into the same trap.

As the days roll into each other, Erin loses track of time. Her world shrinks. Her focus narrows to Fabio and the orbit of people around him. She tells herself it's temporary, that she's doing this for the right reasons, but the truth is harder to face. This isn't just about protecting others or finding closure.

It's about control, about reclaiming a sense of power she hasn't felt since Fabio tore her world apart. Her obsession consumes her, but she doesn't see it that way. To her, this is a necessary act. A way to finally confront the ghost of her past and ensure he can't hurt anyone else.

But with each passing day, Erin loses a little more of herself to the darkness she thought she has escaped. And though she doesn't realise it yet, she's teetering on the edge of a choice that will determine whether she breaks free or gets pulled under once again.

Chapter Eighteen

Erin finally feels she's on the brink of peace, close to walking away from her fixation on Fabio and the hold he still has on her mind. She has been following him for weeks on end, but what she has seen recently has only reassured her that maybe, just maybe, he's not the man he once was.

Today, she watches him enter a solicitor's office downtown, where Gemma is already waiting. The sight of them together—a warm embrace, the kind of closeness that looks genuine—surprises Erin. But what stuns her most is what follows.

Through the office's broad glass windows, Erin sees Fabio meeting with the solicitor, paperwork spread across the table. She watches him sign document after document before handing over a set of keys to Gemma. It's clear what he's doing—he's signing over his entire business to her.

The Fabio she knew would never relinquish control so freely. He thrived on being in charge, on making others dependent on him; never the other way around. Erin can hardly believe what she's witnessing.

For a brief, disorienting moment, she wonders if this is his way of making up for his past—to prove to himself, to

Gemma, and maybe even to some invisible judge in his mind, that he's not that man anymore.

Maybe he's ill, she thinks, *or maybe he's proving his love by making her independent, by giving her control of his life's work.*

It's a gesture so foreign, so uncharacteristic of the man she knows, that Erin's heart softens. She feels an old wound begin to close.

In that moment, she decides she's done. she's ready to walk away from the shadows, to leave Dublin, to rebuild her own life free of this fixation. She knows now that Fabio's life is no longer her business; no longer a reflection of what she has been through or what she needs to prove.

She tells herself she'll pack up and head somewhere new, finally, leaving Fabio—and all that came with him—in the past.

But as she turns to leave, something stops her. Just up the street, she sees Fabio and Gemma stepping out of the office, arm in arm. They pause to chat with a mutual friend.

Erin can't hear what's being said, but she sees Gemma start to laugh at something the friend says, then add her own words with a bright smile, like any other light-hearted conversation. Fabio remains silent beside her, his face tightening just slightly as he looks away.

After they say goodbye to the friend, Erin watches as Fabio's demeanour shifts in an instant. Gone is the attentive partner she has seen moments earlier. He snaps his hand away from Gemma's, his face twists with annoyance.

She's too far away to hear his words, but she sees his mouth moving, his jaw clenching, the look of pure rage in his eyes as he leans down close to Gemma and spits his words into her face. Gemma's expression shifts from surprise to fear in a heartbeat, her head bowing under the weight of his anger.

Erin can tell he's reprimanding her as the words are sharp, his body tense and vibrating with control. As Gemma stammers out an apology, he raises a finger, jabbing it in her face.

It's the same look Erin remembers; that dark, brooding power that once drew her in but later frightened her into silence. She knows what's coming next before it even happens.

Fabio glances around, checking the street, making sure they're out of anyone's view. Then, just as she feared, he grabs Gemma's arm, pulling her close, and with one swift movement, drives his fist into her stomach.

The blow is fast and targeted, and Gemma doubles over in pain, her face twisted in shock and agony. She clutches her stomach, gasping for breath, her eyes wide and glistening with fresh tears.

Her lips move, whispering an apology Erin doesn't need to hear to recognise. She's apologising to him, begging for forgiveness, and the sight makes Erin's blood boil. In that instant, she knows Gemma has been through this before. This isn't a one-time slip or a moment of anger. Fabio hasn't changed—not one bit.

The illusion shatters, and every memory of his rage, his controlling presence, and his manipulation, floods back into her mind. Erin's hands clench into fists at her sides as she watches him mutter something else at Gemma with his expression ice-cold and remorseless.

This is the real Fabio, the man who hides his darkness just long enough to make people believe he has changed, only to unleash it again behind closed doors.

"There he is," she whispers to herself, the bitter realisation cutting through her.

She feels the weight of her history with him settle into her bones. The understanding that his cruelty isn't something he outgrew or left behind. It's part of who he is, woven into his very nature, lurking behind every smile and charming word.

Her mind spins with the knowledge that if she walks away now, Gemma will continue down the same path Erin once did—a path that nearly destroyed her.

A cold resolve settles over her, a sense of purpose she hasn't felt in years. She realises now that walking away isn't an option. She can't let Fabio ruin another innocent girl's life.

For the first time since coming back to Dublin, she knows exactly what she needs to do. She's ready to confront the man who stole her life, not for herself, but for every other woman he might hurt if no one stops him.

Her heart beats heavy with both fear and determination. The memories, once painful and weakening, now fuel her. Fabio's time of hiding behind his charm is over. Erin will make sure of it.

Erin's emotions twist and churn as she stands frozen on Dublin Street, watching Fabio and Gemma disappear down the road. The moment feels suspended in time, every thought, every memory, every regret colliding within her.

Just minutes ago, she had been so close to walking away, ready to put all of this behind her—the stalking, the obsession, the weight of her past. She had convinced herself she was foolish for following him; foolish for believing her gut instincts when everything she observed suggested otherwise.

And now this.

She feels the hot sting of embarrassment rising in her chest. How could she have wasted so much time shadowing Fabio, combing through the details of his life, only to nearly convince herself she was wrong?

All those hours, all that energy spent circling the past like a moth to a flame—what was she thinking? Hadn't she learned her lesson? Hadn't she grown beyond the woman she used to be, the one so consumed by Fabio's world that she forgot to live her own?

Her face flushes as the realisation settles in: she lets herself be fooled. Not by Fabio's charm—no, she saw through that long ago—but by her own doubts. She almost believed the lie he presented, the veneer of change he so skilfully cultivated.

She almost let herself think he is capable of being better, of leaving the darkness behind. And for what? To feel relief? Closure? A pang of shame runs through her as she remembers the fleeting moment of softness she'd felt, watching him sign the gym over to Gemma.

How naive she is to think that gesture, no matter how grand, could undo what she knew in her bones.

But then, that same shame she is feeling, shame she has felt many times before morphs into something sharper. Anger. At herself, at him, at everything. She's angry for letting herself be pulled into this mess, angry for doubting her instincts, angry for the part of her that had *wanted* him to have changed.

Because even though it hurts, even though it churns up old wounds, she *wants* to be wrong about Fabio. She wants to believe that time can soften people, that they can heal, grow, and leave the worst parts of themselves behind. That belief—however, small and fleeting—feels foolish now.

But there's also a darker, more conflicted emotion creeping through her: satisfaction. Not happiness, not relief, but a grim, hollow sense of vindication. She *was* right. Her gut has been screaming at her for weeks, telling her that Fabio hasn't changed, that his charm is a façade.

And now, watching Gemma bow under the weight of his anger, flinching at his touch, Erin knows she never should have doubted herself. She had seen this play out before, lived it, survived it—and there it is again, unfolding right in front of her like a scene from her own life.

The satisfaction feels wrong, like a betrayal of her better self. She's not happy that she is right—how could she be? What she's seen is nothing to be happy about. Fabio hasn't changed, and the proof of that lies in Gemma's pain.

The way in which she clutches her stomach and whispers apologies for something that isn't her fault. But the satisfaction isn't about Fabio or Gemma. It's about Erin. It's about the fact that her instincts, her hard-won intuition, hadn't failed her.

Still, that vindication is a double-edged sword. Knowing she is right also means knowing that Gemma is trapped in the same nightmare that Erin escaped from. It means that Fabio is still dangerous, still wielding his power to control and harm. And it means that Erin can't just walk away.

Her anger, her shame, her vindication—they all converge into a cold relentless determination. Fabio's mask has slipped, and now Erin can see him for exactly what he is: the same man she left behind, only older, more polished and practised.

And Gemma is the new version of herself—young, hopeful, unguarded. The thought makes Erin's stomach churn.

As much as she wants to berate herself for wasting time, for allowing herself to get drawn back into Fabio's orbit, she knows now that it isn't time wasted. Her obsession, misguided as it may have been, led her to this moment. She's no longer chasing ghosts or looking for closure. This isn't about her anymore.

It's about Gemma.

It's about stopping Fabio before he can hurt her—or anyone else—the way he hurt Erin. And while a part of her feels a sick, bitter satisfaction in knowing she was right about him all along, another part of her wishes desperately that she has been wrong. If only for Gemma's sake.

Chapter Nineteen

Erin keeps close to Fabio as he moves through the city, staying just far enough behind to avoid detection. Her breath is steady and her steps quiet, as she watches him navigate the familiar streets. The Dublin air is damp and cold, but she hardly notices.

Her focus is sharp, her instincts primed. When he finally reaches his apartment and disappears inside, she assumes he's in for the night. Yet, just as she's about to turn away, she sees him reappear, slipping out of the building with a sense of urgency.

Her brow furrows. Nearly midnight, and he's heading towards the gym? The question gnaws at her as she follows him through the quiet streets, her unease deepening with each step.

Fabio's movements are purposeful, almost calculated. This isn't a casual stroll, and she knows better than to dismiss the tingling in her gut.

When they near the gym, Erin's eyes catch on a sleek black Mercedes parked by the kerb. A tall man steps out of the car, his figure broad and imposing. Even in the dim light, he radiates danger. Fabio greets him with a nod, and together they disappear inside, locking the door behind them.

Erin edges closer, her curiosity blazing now. She crouches by the front window, her breath fogging the glass as she peers inside.

She can see them heading straight to the back office, their movements smooth and confident, like men who know exactly what they're doing. Fabio opens a drawer and pulls out a small, plastic-wrapped bundle. Erin's stomach twists as realisation dawns—it's drugs.

Her jaw tightens as she watches the exchange. Fabio hands the bundle over, and in return, the other man places a thick stack of cash on the desk. The whole scene plays out with unsettling ease as if this is routine for them.

Erin's mind races, piecing together the puzzle. The gym isn't the hard-earned business he'd always claimed it to be—it's a front; a cover for his operation.

And Gemma. Erin's stomach churns at the thought. The transfer of ownership to Gemma wasn't about love or partnership; it was insurance. If the operation goes south, Fabio could walk away clean, leaving Gemma to take the fall.

The realisation makes Erin's blood boil. Fabio hasn't changed—not even a little. If anything, he has become more deceitful, weaving a web of lies to protect himself while pulling others into his schemes.

Her hands routinely clench into fists, a habit she inherited from years of fighting. Gemma doesn't know the truth. She's being used; set up to be a scapegoat, and Fabio doesn't seem to care. The thought stirs something deep and primal in Erin. A fierce, protective instinct flares within her, igniting a fire she hasn't felt in a while.

This is her chance. She can hurt him—not just physically, but in a way that will truly wound him. She can expose his lies, dismantle the life he has so carefully built, and make him pay for everything he's done.

Under the cover of darkness, Erin pulls a black balaclava over her head. The wool is rough against her skin, but she relishes the feeling. It's a symbol, a transformation.

Tonight, she isn't Erin O'Connor, the Irish Invincible. Tonight, she's faceless, a shadow moving through the night. Justice personified.

She waits in the alley near the gym, her body coils with anticipation. The minutes stretch on, each one sharpening her focus. When the black Mercedes finally pulls away, her heart kicks into a faster rhythm. She moves closer to the gym entrance, blending with the shadows.

Fabio emerges a few minutes later, his head down as he fumbles with his keys. Erin doesn't hesitate. She steps out of the darkness, her fist flying with unerring precision. The impact sends a jolt through her arm, but the sound of her knuckles meeting his jaw is deeply satisfying. Fabio stumbles, a look of shock flashing across his face.

Before he can react, she strikes again. Her years of training take over, every movement is honed and lethal. Each punch connects with brutal efficiency, driving him to the ground.

Fabio barely has time to raise a hand in defence before he sprawls on the pavement, blood trickling from his split lip.

Erin stands over him, her chest heaving. Adrenaline courses through her veins, a heady rush that makes her feel alive. It's a buzz, electric and intoxicating, and she wants more. She crouches down, rifling through his pockets with steady hands. His keys. His wallet. She takes them both, her mind racing as she slips inside the gym.

The office is exactly as she saw it through the window. The drawer is still open, the stack of cash sitting there like an invitation. Erin grabs it without hesitation, savouring the thrill of taking from him what he's stolen from so many others.

She pauses for a moment, letting the weight of what she's done sink in. This isn't just about revenge—it's about reclaiming her power and taking back the control Fabio once stole from her.

The thought sends another rush of adrenaline surging through her, and she feels a small, triumphant smile tug at her lips.

On her way out, she steps over Fabio's unconscious form. She doesn't linger—just long enough to toss his wallet back onto the ground. She wants it to look like a mugging, something random and brutal.

Fabio has enemies, and she knows losing the drug money will send them after him faster than anything else.

As she disappears into the night, her pulse still racing, Erin feels a strange sense of exhilaration. For the first time in God knows how long, she feels truly alive. This isn't just revenge—it's justice. It's a reckoning.

And as she vanishes into the darkness, she knows Fabio's torment is only beginning. The thought fuels her steps, a quiet triumph swelling in her chest. She's done being a victim. Now, she's the one in control.

As Erin strides through the quiet Dublin streets, the rush of adrenaline begins to ebb, leaving her mind sharper, and clearer. She replays the events of the night in her head, savouring the memory of Fabio being sprawled on the pavement—stunned and broken.

A small, grim satisfaction tugs at her again, as she imagines what must be going through his mind when he wakes up to discover the money gone. She knows Fabio too well to think he's running this operation alone. He has always been the kind of man who talks big and struts around like he's in charge, but she has seen the truth.

Fabio doesn't have the brains—or the guts—to mastermind something like this. No, he's just a cog in a larger machine, a middleman at best. And whoever is pulling the strings above him, isn't going to be happy. The thought gives Erin an undeniable thrill.

She pictures the moment when Fabio's boss finds out what happened. The fury. The disbelief. The cold, calculating anger that follows. She imagines them demanding answers. Their patience razor-thin as they grill Fabio about how he managed to lose a significant sum of money in one night.

Fabio, sweating bullets, will try to explain. He'll stumble over his words, feeding them half-truths and outright lies, but it won't matter. She knows men like Fabio's boss. They don't care about excuses—they care about results. And Fabio has failed. Erin smirks to herself as she envisions the fallout.

She can almost see it: Fabio being summoned to a dimly lit room, his bravado crumbling under the weight of their expectations. He'll try to play it cool, but the fear in his eyes will give him away. And when they demand repayment, he'll have nothing to offer. No money. No plan. Just empty promises. And that's when things will turn ugly.

Erin's steps are slow as the image solidifies in her mind. She knows what happens to men who lose money in this line of work. They don't get a slap on the wrist or a second chance. They get punished—publicly and violently, as an example to everyone else. She can already picture Fabio's face; bruised and bloodied, his arrogant smirk replaced by sheer terror.

For a moment, a flicker of pity tries to surface. She pushes it down immediately. Fabio brought this on himself. He made his choices, just like she has made hers. And he has hurt too many people, and used too many women like Gemma, to deserve her sympathy now.

Her mind drifts back to Fabio's boss. What kind of man would entrust someone like Fabio with that much cash? She pictures a shadowy figure—someone cold, ruthless and meticulous. Someone, who doesn't tolerate failure. And Fabio, with his flimsy excuses and lack of foresight, will be no match for him.

"Let him sweat," she mutters under her breath, the words slipping out before she realises it.

The thought of Fabio scrambling to cover his tracks—to scrape together enough money to pay back what he has lost—is deliciously satisfying. He'll be running scared, looking over his shoulder, waiting for the hammer to drop. And when it does, Erin hopes it's swift and brutal.

As she rounds the corner to her flat, her thoughts slow, but the buzz remains. She knows this isn't over—not yet. Fabio's downfall is only beginning, and she plans to watch it unfold from a distance. She waited for years to see him pay for his lies, and his betrayals, and now, she finally has the power to make it happen.

A wave of satisfaction settles over Erin as she drifts off to sleep that night, a deep and undisturbed rest she has been long overdue. She sleeps through until dawn, letting herself bask in the sense of vengeance served, however, brief.

Chapter Twenty

The next morning, with a quiet resolve, she slips out and makes her way to Fabio's apartment. Her plan is simple: wait, watch, and see the fallout unfold as his associates realise what has happened. He is set to lose both his money and his reputation—a small but fitting revenge.

Erin waits, every nerve on edge, as she thinks about what could unfold in the coming hours. She can practically see it in her mind: the enforcers showing up, the questions, and Fabio stammering his way through flimsy excuses. It is only a matter of time, she is certain.

What Erin doesn't realise is that Fabio had been forced to spend the night in the hospital. The mugging was brutal enough to warrant scans and monitoring for a potential concussion. Fabio had no choice but to endure the indignity of being patched up like a broken man.

Even as she relishes his suffering, Erin feels the creeping weight of unease, but she is determined to find out for herself what the fallout will look like.

Late in the morning, she watches as Gemma's car pulls up. Erin's breath hitches as Gemma steps out, helping Fabio from the passenger seat. He leans heavily on her, his arm slung over her shoulders, his face swollen and purple with bruises.

Erin notes the stiffness in his movements, and the careful way he walks, as though every step sends a jolt of pain through his body.

For a moment, she feels a flicker of satisfaction.

"Look at you now, Fabio," she says to herself.

The arrogant swagger is gone, replaced by a limping, beaten man who has to rely on someone else just to make it inside.

As the hours pass, though, her expectations begin to shift. She keeps waiting, wondering when the inevitable confrontation will come, but there is nothing—no enforcers, no police, no pounding on the door. Something feels wrong, a gnawing feeling that twists in her stomach.

She watches the shadows lengthen, her instincts beginning to thrum with unease. Then, just after dusk, she sees movement at the door. Fabio emerges, but there is something different.

The bruises are still there, his gait unsteady, but his hands are smeared with dark stains as if he has been scrubbing at something that wouldn't come clean. Erin's heart clenches as she recognises the telltale marks of blood, dried and dark on his knuckles.

"Oh no…Gemma," she whispers, horror dawning in her eyes.

Erin doesn't hesitate. Her feet carry her across the street before she even realises that she is moving. Her pulse thunders in her ears as she reaches the apartment door, and her hand is trembling as she turns the knob. It isn't locked. The door swings open, revealing a scene of chaos inside.

Broken glass glitters on the floor, reflecting the dim light like shards of ice. Furniture lies overturned, and the room is a picture of violence and destruction. And then, Erin sees her.

"Gemma," she whispered, her voice breaking as she dropped to her knees beside the young woman.

Gemma lay crumpled on the living room floor; her breath is shallow and uneven. Bruises bloom across her face and arms, angry purples and blues that stand out starkly against her pale skin.

Her lip is split, a thin trickle of blood drying at the corner of her mouth, and her eyelids flutter weakly as Erin gently touches her shoulder.

"Gemma, can you hear me?" Erin's voice trembled; her throat tight with panic.

A faint groan escapes Gemma's lips, her head lolling to the side. Erin bites back a sob, her guilt crashes over her in waves. This is her fault. She has set this in motion. Her actions, and her need for revenge have put Gemma in harm's way.

Tears sting her eyes as she fumbles for her phone, her hands shaking so badly that it takes her three tries to dial the emergency number. She forces herself to stay calm as she gives the address, her voice flat and clipped despite the turmoil inside her.

"Send an ambulance. Please, hurry."

She ends the call and sits back, her hands trembling as she looks down at Gemma. She wants to stay, to make sure she is okay, but she knows she can't. If the medics or police find her here, it will raise questions she isn't ready to answer.

Erin stands, her heart breaking as she looks at Gemma one last time. "You'll be okay," she whispers, more to herself than to Gemma. "You have to be okay."

She slips out of the apartment just as the distant wail of sirens cuts through the night. From the shadows across the street, she watches as the medics arrive, rushing inside and carefully lifting Gemma onto a stretcher.

Her chest tightens as she sees the young woman's limp form being carried out, her face is bruised and bloodied. The sight will haunt Erin, she knows it will.

As the ambulance pulls away, sirens fade into the distance, and Erin stands frozen in the cold night air. Guilt twists in her gut, sharp and unforgiving. She wants to bring Fabio down, but she didn't mean for this to happen. She never meant for Gemma to pay the price.

Her jaw tightens as a new resolve hardens within her. This isn't over—not by a long shot. Fabio has crossed a line, and now it isn't just about revenge. It is about justice. It is about making sure no one else suffers under his control.

She turns and disappears into the night, her mind racing with a new plan. Fabio has to be stopped. This time, she will make sure it is for good.

Chapter Twenty-One

Erin has spent years wrestling with her past, haunted by the choices she has made and the ones that had been made for her. Yet, as she crouches in the shadows outside the gym that night, she feels a clarity she hasn't experienced in a long time.

The events of the past few days have crystallised her thoughts into a single, unavoidable truth: Fabio can't be allowed to continue. Not after what he has done to Gemma, not after what he had done to her, and certainly not with the shadow of what he might do to the next unsuspecting person.

Erin is acting off intuition, this wasn't part of her plan. Her goal had been to destroy Fabio's reputation, to dismantle his life in a way that would expose his true nature to everyone who believed in his carefully constructed façade. But that plan feels small now—inadequate.

Fabio dodged another bullet by being presented with a free pass by his drug boss, who isn't worried about losing the money. In that line of business, it's always best to factor in taking a hit now and then, and he isn't going to hold Fabio responsible.

Gemma's battered face is burned into Erin's mind, a visceral reminder of how dangerous Fabio truly is.

She spent the night replaying everything while pacing in her small flat as she tried to reconcile her need for justice with the growing realisation that justice—in the traditional sense—might never come. Fabio has spent his entire life evading consequences.

He knows how to cover his tracks. How to manipulate people and systems to his advantage. If she exposes him, he'll find a way to slip through the cracks, just as he always has.

Erin can't let that happen.

In her fractured, desperate mind, she begins to convince herself that killing Fabio isn't just an act of vengeance—it is a necessity. She tells herself it isn't about her anger or her need for closure; it is about protecting others.

Gemma might recover from her injuries, but what about the next woman Fabio manipulates? The next person who crosses him and pays the price? He is a disease, spreading harm wherever he goes, and Erin sees herself as the only one willing to put an end to it.

By the time she tracks him to the gym, her resolve is absolute. There is no room for doubt, no second-guessing. She has spent the day watching him, waiting for the right moment, ensuring that Gemma is safe in the hospital before she makes her move. Now, it's time.

When she steps into the gym, her footsteps light and deliberate, she doesn't feel like the woman she was just days ago. She feels like someone else entirely—someone with purpose. Someone, who can finally finish what started all those years ago.

Fabio is on the bench, oblivious to her presence, his focus on the weights in his hands. Erin moves quietly and stands over him, her shadow falls across his face.

The moment his eyes meet hers, she sees it—the flicker of fear, the dawning realisation that she isn't there to talk. There is no balaclava this time. She wants him to know, to see her, and to understand that this is the end.

As she presses her hands down on the barbell, the weight slams into his throat with a dull, unforgiving thud. Fabio's eyes widen in shock, his body instinctively thrashing as he tries to push the bar off him, but his wrists are pinned.

Erin leans her full weight onto the bar, her muscles burning with the effort, but she doesn't let up.

The gym fills with the sound of his choking gasps, the desperate, panic noises of a man who suddenly realises he isn't in control. Erin's mind is a storm of emotions—rage, satisfaction, sorrow—but above all, there is a grim sense of purpose.

This is for Gemma, she thinks to herself. *This is for me. This is for every person you've hurt and every person you could have hurt.*

Fabio's struggles grow weaker, his movements slowing as the life drains from his body. Erin's arms tremble with the effort, but she holds firm, her jaw clenches as she forces herself to see it through. When his body is finally still, she lets go, stepping back as the barbell rests motionless across his throat.

Her chest heaves as she stares down at him, her mind spinning. She tells herself it will look like an accident—a freak incident that can happen to anyone lifting weights alone. She makes sure of it; arranging the scene just so before she leaves.

But deep down, she knows this isn't about making it look like an accident. It is about taking control, about ensuring that Fabio can never hurt anyone again.

As she steps out into the cool night air, a strange sense of calm settles over her. The adrenaline still coursing through her veins, but it is accompanied by something else: relief. Fabio is gone, and with him, the weight of years of fear and anger seems to lift from her shoulders.

But Erin knows her work isn't done. She can't move forward until she is certain Gemma is safe. That is her next stop—back to the hospital, where she will watch from a distance, ensuring that Gemma is cared for and protected.

As she walks through the empty streets, her thoughts churn. She tells herself over and over that she has done what needed to be done, and that the world is better off without Fabio in it. But deep down, a small, quiet part of her wonders if she has crossed a line she could never uncross.

Shaking the thought away, Erin straightens her shoulders and quickens her pace. Fabio is gone and the future is finally hers to shape. Now, all that matters is making sure the people he has hurt can heal—starting with Gemma.

Chapter Twenty-Two

Gemma takes a deep breath before stepping into the gym. She builds up to this moment for days, torn between painful memories of Fabio and the idea that maybe this place could now hold something different—something good.

Gemma hesitates at the threshold, gripping the strap of her gym bag as if it were a lifeline. The door creaks faintly as she nudges it open, letting the familiar smell of the gym wash over her.

Her eyes dart to the faint scuff marks on the rubber matting and the equipment arranged with cold precision. It still feels like *his* space.

Fabio's presence clings to the gym like a ghost, his shadow lingering in every corner and every mirrored wall. Gemma wants to feel relief that he is gone, but her emotions are a tangled mess of guilt, anger, and confusion.

As she steps further inside, she notices a figure in the centre of the room. The woman standing is tall and broad-shouldered with her hands on her hips, scanning the gym with a critical eye. There is something in her stance—self-assured yet wary—that makes Gemma pause.

The woman turns at the sound of the door, and her sharp eyes land on Gemma. For a heartbeat, neither speak. Then

Gemma's breath catches in her throat. The scars are unmistakable, a testament to a life hard lived. Even if they hadn't been there, Gemma would have recognised that face.

"You're…the Irish Invincible," Gemma whispers, her voice shaky.

It isn't just a title—it is a legend. Erin had been a powerhouse in the fighting world, a name that commanded both respect and fear. And she is also someone Gemma have never hoped to meet.

Erin's lips curve into a wry smile, tinged with weariness. "Not anymore," she said, her Irish accent softened by time. "I'm just Erin now."

The air between them is heavy, thick with a shared history that neither has anticipated confronting today. Fabio has been the thread that connected them—Gemma, the partner he has broken down piece by piece, and Erin, the ex he left in his destructive wake.

Both women have survived him in different ways, though survival hasn't come without scars.

Gemma crosses her arms, more out of instinct than defence, and forces out a dry laugh.

"So, what am I supposed to do with a bloody gym?" she asks, gesturing around at the space Fabio has left her like an unwanted inheritance.

Her voice carries a note of bitterness she can't quite hide.

Erin steps forward, her movements are deliberate, and she stops a few paces away.

"Actually," she said, her voice steady but laced with an undercurrent of intensity, "that's why I'm here."

Gemma blinks, confused.

Erin reaches into the leather bag slung over her shoulder and pulls out a thick stack of cash. She holds it out, her gaze unwavering.

"I'm looking for a space. Somewhere, I can teach self-defence to women. A place where they can feel safe. Where they can learn to stand their ground, to be strong enough to face whatever comes at them." She pauses, letting her words sink in before adding, "We could turn this place into that. Would you be interested?"

Gemma let out a long breath. Her gaze shifts between Erin and the cash, her thoughts racing. She doesn't know this woman beyond her reputation and the unspoken bond of surviving Fabio. But there was a certainty in Erin's eyes that makes her want to believe in something—maybe even herself.

"So, what do you say?" Erin asks, her voice gentler now. "Take the money. Turn this place into something better. It doesn't have to be his anymore. It can be *yours*. Ours even, if you're willing to give it a shot."

The idea seems almost too big, too impossible. And yet.

Gemma reaches out slowly, her fingers brushing the edge of the stack before she grips it firmly. It is heavier than she expected, but in her hands, it feels like something more than just cash. It felt like the weight of a new beginning.

"Yes," she said, the word more resolute than she'd anticipated. "I think I'd be more than interested."

Erin can still sense a tinge of reluctance in Gemma, and she doesn't want to force her into something that isn't for her.

Erin gestures to the gym, her expression is filled with purpose. "This place can be more than what Fabio left behind. It can be a sanctuary. A place where women learn to fight, to protect themselves. A place where they both realise, they're worth more than the lies men like him feed them."

Gemma raises an eyebrow, scepticism creeping in. "You really think a gym can do all that?"

Erin smiled faintly, a hint of steel in her gaze. "I know it can. I've seen it happen. When you teach a woman to defend herself, you're not just teaching her how to block a punch or throw one back. You're giving her the tools to stand tall, to feel strong enough to walk away from what's hurting her. And for some women, that can mean everything."

She begins to pace, her movements fluid, the words coming faster now as her vision unfolds. "We can offer classes—self-defence, fitness, even support groups. We can bring in counsellors, people who know how to help women heal, not just physically but mentally.

"This gym can be a place where they feel safe for the first time in their lives. Where they can rebuild what men like Fabio try to tear down."

Gemma listens, the walls around her crumbling piece by piece. Erin's vision is bold, but there is something about the way she speaks that makes it feel possible.

Erin stopped pacing, turning back to Gemma. "And it's not just about protecting women from men like Fabio," she said, her voice quieter but no less fierce. "It's about teaching them that they don't have to be victims. That they can take back control, even when it feels impossible."

Gemma let out a shaky breath, the weight of it all sinking in. Fabio's ghost still lingers, but Erin's words feel like a lifeline; a way to push back against everything he had left behind. She looks around the gym, seeing it not as it was but as it could be—a space filled with women who were stronger, freer and more resilient than they'd ever thought possible.

She glanced back at Erin, her decision clear. "If we do this," she said, her voice steady, "it has to be about more than just self-defence. It has to be about giving them something they can carry with them. Strength. Confidence. Hope."

Erin nodded, a flicker of a smile crossing her face. "Exactly."

Gemma takes a deep breath, her hand tightening around the money once more. For the first time, it didn't feel like blood money anymore to Erin. It felt like a beginning.

"All right," Gemma said, meeting Erin's gaze with a spark of determination. "Let's do it."

Erin extends her hand, and Gemma takes it without hesitation. Their handshake is firm, charged with an unspoken promise.

Together, they will turn the gym into more than a building. It will be a place where women can rise above their pain, where they can reclaim their power and rewrite their stories.

For Gemma and Erin, it isn't just about the gym. It is about something far greater—a chance to finally break free of the chains Fabio left behind and to help others do the same.

As they stand in the centre of the gym, the faint hum of possibility fills the air. And now the space no longer felt haunted. It felt alive.

Chapter Twenty-Three

The gym has become a second home—not just for the women who train there, but for Erin and Gemma as well. It is a space alive with energy and transformation, where every punch thrown or technique learned, carries a deeper meaning. Women walk in hunched with burdens and leave a little taller and a little stronger.

The success of the gym is undeniable. Donations roll steadily in, thanks to local businesses that believe in their mission, and the waiting list for classes continues to grow.

Gemma has even started dreaming about expanding into the unused upstairs space, turning it into a dedicated area for counselling sessions and support groups.

Erin and Gemma have grown inseparable, their bond is forged not just by shared trauma, but by their shared vision for the gym. They laugh, bicker and celebrate every small victory together.

For Erin, it is a revelation. She never had someone she could lean on like this. Someone, who understands her—flaws and all—and still stands by her side.

"You know," Erin said one afternoon as they sat on the gym's front steps, drinking coffee after a packed Saturday class, "I think you might be the closest thing I've ever had to a sister."

Gemma chuckled, nudging her shoulder. "Well, you're stuck with me now, so you better get used to it."

But as Gemma laughs, Erin's stomach twists. She isn't used to this kind of closeness. The depth of their friendship should have been comforting, but instead, it gnaws at her. The guilt is growing harder to ignore.

Fabio.

The name still echoes in her mind, tethering her to the darkest parts of her past. The truth about his death—and her role in it—is a constant weight on her chest. And the stalking, the months she had spent watching Gemma and Fabio from a distance; trying to find a way to confront him, to end the cycle of destruction he left in his wake.

She has convinced herself that keeping quiet is for the best. That Gemma didn't need to know.

But now?

Now, it feels like she is lying every time she looks into Gemma's eyes.

One late evening, after everyone else has gone home, Erin finds herself lingering in the main room of the gym. The fluorescent lights hum softly overhead, and the mats are still warm from the bodies that have trained on them throughout the day.

Gemma is across the room, tidying up the rack of kettlebells, humming a tune under her breath. Erin watches her for a moment, feeling the familiar pang of guilt twist in her chest.

"Gemma," she said finally, her voice softer than usual.

Gemma looks up with a curious smile on her face. "Yeah?"

"I need to talk to you. About...Fabio."

The name hit the air like a stone, heavy and unwelcome. Gemma's smile fades, and she straightens. Her expression is wary.

"What about him?"

Erin hesitates, her hands clenching at her sides. This is it. There is no going back once she says the words.

"I haven't been completely honest with you," Erin began, her voice trembling. "About what happened to him. About how he died."

Gemma freeze, her brow furrowing. "What are you talking about? It was an accident. They told me—"

"It wasn't," Erin interrupted, her voice breaking. "It wasn't an accident, Gemma. I killed him."

The silence that follows is suffocating. Gemma stares at Erin, her face a mixture of confusion and disbelief.

"What?" she whispers, her voice barely audible.

Erin forces herself to continue. "I went to confront him that day. I'd been...following him. Watching him, trying to figure out how to stop him from hurting anyone else. I saw what he was doing to you, and I couldn't stand by anymore."

Gemma takes a step back, shaking her head. "You were *stalking* us?"

"I didn't know what else to do," Erin admitted, desperation creeping into her tone. "I saw the bruises, the way he controlled you. I knew what he was capable of. I wanted to protect you."

Gemma's eyes narrowed, anger beginning to simmer beneath her shock. "Protect me? By killing him?"

"I didn't set out to kill him, I just felt that he left me no choice," Erin said quickly. "And I...staged it to look like an accident."

Gemma stares at her, her chest rising and falling rapidly. "So, you lied to me," she said, her voice trembling with anger. "All this time, you let me think it was an accident. You let me mourn him, grieve him—"

"Gemma, please," Erin said, stepping closer. "I didn't know how to tell you. I thought it would hurt you more to know the truth."

"Hurt me more?" Gemma's voice rose, her eyes flashing. "Do you have any idea what it's like to live with this? To wonder if I could have done something different if I could have stopped it?"

Erin flinch. "I'm sorry," she said, her voice cracking. "I thought I was doing the right thing."

Gemma shakes her head, her anger spilling over. "And the stalking? How long were you watching us, Erin? How long were you spying on my life?"

Erin hesitates, and the pause is the answer enough.

Gemma lets out a bitter laugh, tears streaming down her face. "You're unbelievable. You act like you're this righteous crusader, saving women from men like Fabio. But you're just as manipulative as he was."

Erin recoils as if she's been slapped. "That's not fair," she said, her voice shaking. "I was trying to help you."

"Help me?" Gemma's voice is sharp, her words cutting like glass. "You destroyed everything. Do you think I wanted this? To carry the weight of someone's death on my shoulders? To lose any chance of closure?"

Erin's eyes are filling with tears. "I didn't know what else to do," she said quietly. "I'm so sorry, Gemma. For everything."

Gemma turns away, her arms are crossed tightly over her chest. "I need some time," she said, her voice cold. "I don't know if I can do this anymore. Any of it."

"Gemma, please," Erin said, stepping forward. "We can work through this. Don't let this ruin what we've built."

But Gemma didn't respond. She grabs her bag and walks out of the gym, leaving Erin standing alone in the empty room.

The days that followed are a blur. Gemma stopped answering Erin's calls and texts, leaving her messages unanswered. Erin kept the gym running as best as she could, but without Gemma, it felt hollow.

The women who train there, notice the tension, the unspoken shift in the air. Erin tries to keep up appearances, but she can't shake the feeling that everything is unravelling.

When Gemma finally returns to the gym a week later, her expression is guarded. She avoids Erin's gaze, focusing on the classes and paperwork with a detached efficiency.

Erin gives her space, unsure of how to fix what has been broken.

But as the days turned into weeks, Erin begins to realise that the bond they shared—the sisterhood that means so much to her—might never be the same. And for the first time, she wonders if her decision to tell the truth has cost her more than she was prepared to lose.

Gemma can't look at Erin the same way anymore. The woman who has become her closest friend, her sister-in-arms, now carries a shadow that Gemma couldn't ignore. Every laugh they'd shared, every victory they'd celebrated at the gym, felt tainted by the weight of Erin's confession.

Every time Erin walks into the gym, Gemma feels her chest tighten. The betrayal runs deep, not just because of the lies, but because Erin has taken away her agency, her chance to confront Fabio on her own terms. Gemma isn't sure if she can forgive her. Or if she even wants to try.

One evening, after the last class has wrapped up, Erin approaches Gemma, her shoulders are slumped in a way that is so unlike her.

"Can we talk?" Erin asked quietly.

Gemma nods, crossing her arms defensively as they step into the small office at the back of the gym.

"I'm leaving," Erin said, her voice steady, though her eyes betrayed her unease.

Gemma blinks, the words taking her by surprise. "Leaving? What do you mean?"

"I think it's best," Erin said. "For both of us. You don't trust me anymore, and I don't blame you. I need to figure some things out. I need to…face what I've done."

Gemma feels a lump rise in her throat but forces it down. "You're right," she said, her voice tight. "Maybe some distance is a good idea."

Erin nods, her gaze is fixed on the floor. "I just want you to know that I'm sorry. For everything. I never wanted to hurt you."

Gemma doesn't respond, and after a long, tense silence, Erin turns and walks out of the office, leaving Gemma standing alone.

What Gemma didn't know—what Erin couldn't bring herself to say—is where she is really going.

The following morning, Erin walks into a Garda station and confesses everything. She tells them about Fabio, about the confrontation, about the staged accident. She leaves nothing out. For the first time since that fateful day, she feels a strange sense of peace.

When she is arrested and placed in a holding cell, she thinks of Gemma. Will she hate her for this too? Or will she understand? Erin doesn't know, but she is done running from the truth.

Gemma finds out through the news. She is sitting on her couch, stunned, as the headline scrolls across the screen:

"Former UFC Champion and Local Gym Founder Arrested for Involuntary Manslaughter in Connection with Fabio Silva's Death."

Her hands shake as she dials Erin's number, only to realise it won't connect. Without hesitation, she drives to the station, demanding to see her. It isn't until the next day when Erin has been transferred to the detention centre, that she is allowed a visit.

When Gemma enters the sterile room, separated from Erin by a pane of glass, her emotions overflow. Erin looks smaller somehow, sitting in the jumpsuit, her face pale but calm.

"Why?" Gemma says as soon as she picks up the receiver. "Why did you do this?"

Erin's voice came through the receiver, soft but steady. "Because it was the right thing to do. I've been carrying this for too long, Gemma. I couldn't lie anymore. You deserved better than that."

Gemma's eyes are filled with tears. "I didn't want this. I didn't want you to go to jail for a scumbag like Fabio."

"I know," Erin said. "But I needed to do it. For me. For you. For every woman he would have hurt if I hadn't stopped him."

Gemma presses her hand against the glass. "I forgive you," she said, her voice breaking. "For everything. I don't hate you, Erin. I could never hate you."

A tear slips down Erin's cheek, but she smiles. "Thank you. That means more than you know."

Chapter Twenty-Four

When Erin's case goes to trial, the court takes into account her honesty, her lack of intent to kill, and the circumstances surrounding Fabio's abusive behaviour. The judge sentences her to seven years, with the final three years suspended.

As the verdict is read, Erin feels a strange mix of relief and resignation. She will serve her time, but she will finally be free of the lies and guilt that have haunted her for so long.

Prison is different this time. Erin has spent years fearing it, imagining the worst, but the reality is surprising. The guards treat her with respect, and even the other inmates seem to admire her. Many of the women inside there, have their own stories of abuse, and Erin's actions—flawed as they are—resonates with them.

Within weeks, Erin finds a new purpose. She takes a job as a trainer in the prison gym, teaching fitness classes and self-defence techniques. For the first time in ages, she feels like she is making a real difference again, even behind bars.

She also avails of the prison counselling services; something she had never realised she needed before, even though she made it available to her gym goers.

Her days fall into a steady rhythm, and though she misses her freedom, she finds a kind of solace in the routine.

One day, several months into her sentence, Erin is surprised to learn she has a visitor. She expects it to be Gemma as usual, but when she walks into the visitation room, she stops in her tracks.

Callum.

The boy she'd met at 15 during her summer in the Gaeltacht. The boy who had once made her laugh until her sides ached. Now a man, he sat across the table, his hair a little longer, his face more lined, but his eyes just as kind.

"I didn't think you'd remember me," Erin said as she sat down, her voice barely above a whisper.

Callum smiled. "I've never forgotten you. I heard about…everything. I just wanted to see how you were doing."

They talk for hours, catching up on years of life. Callum tells her about his job, his travels, and how he'd often thought about reaching out to her but never found the right time.

Erin listens, astonished. She hasn't expected anyone from her past to come back into her life, let alone someone who made such a deep impression on her years ago.

"I've been thinking about you ever since that summer," Callum confesses, his voice low. "You were always so strong, shy, but sure of yourself. I admired that. I still do."

Erin smiles softly; the first genuine smile she feels in months. She hasn't realised how much she has missed having someone like Callum around. Someone, who sees her for who she truly is, without the layers of guilt and shame she has wrapped herself in.

From that moment on, Callum visits her every week. He comes with stories about the world outside, about the people they both knew and about the things that have changed. He brings her books, flowers, anything that might brighten her day.

The connection between them grew. It isn't just the old bond from their youth, but something deeper. Erin begins to open up to him: about her past, about Fabio, about her time in prison, and about the mistakes she's made. And he listens. Without judgment.

Each visit feels like a small piece of her past healing. For the first time since Gemma, she feels like she isn't alone in the world. Callum's unwavering support gives her strength. He is the lifeline she never knew she needed.

After nearly three years of serving her sentence, Erin is eligible for early release, and that release day has finally arrived. The prison gates open, and she steps out into the world, breathing in the fresh air, and feeling the sun on her face. It is an odd feeling like she is waking up from a long, dark dream.

Callum is waiting for her, standing by the gates with a bouquet of wildflowers in his hands. His smile is the same, warm and familiar one she remembers, and at that moment, it feels like no time has passed at all.

"Ready for your new life?" he asked, his voice playful yet sincere.

Erin nodded, her heart full. "I don't know where it will go but, hopefully, I can stay out of trouble this time."

They walk side by side, leaving the prison behind. Callum's arm is around her shoulders—a comforting presence. They don't need to talk much. The silence between them is peaceful, a reflection of everything Erin has been through, and everything they are about to build together.

As they sit down on a set of steps in a quiet park, the world feels right. Erin leans her head on Callum's shoulder, her breath steady, her body at ease for the first time in years. Callum's arm is wrapped around her, pulling her close.

"I'm glad you're here," Erin whispered.

"Always," Callum replied softly, squeezing her shoulder.

They sit together, watching the sunset, knowing that whatever comes next, they will face it together. The weight of Erin's past is still there, but it no longer controls her.

The truth has set her free in more ways than one. Now, she can finally look forward to the future. To a life built on second chances, trust, and the love of someone who truly understands her.

Epilogue
The Irish Invincible

The cool Donegal breeze sweeps over Erin as she stands on the rocky cliffs overlooking the Atlantic Ocean. Below her, the waves crash against the jagged shoreline, their rhythmic sound is like a soothing backdrop to the life she has built.

Gweedore stretches out behind her, a place of raw beauty and resilience, much like herself. This rugged corner of the world has become home in every sense of the word.

It has been a little over two years since she and Callum had left Dublin to settle here, leaving behind the chaos of the past for the serenity of Donegal. Callum, with his easy laugh and steadfast heart, has been her anchor through the transition.

They have chosen Gweedore together—a place that held good memories for both of them, a place where the air felt lighter and life simpler.

The people of Gweedore had embraced Erin without hesitation. This is a community that understands pain, that carries its own scars, and yet, somehow, always finds a way to stand tall.

They heard whispers of her past, the battles she had fought, and the sacrifices she had made. To them, Erin isn't just a survivor—she is a hero.

The day she opened her gym, *The Invincible*, the small town turned out in force. Locals of all ages come to see the woman who lives up to the name. The woman who brings hope and strength to others even while carrying her own burdens.

The gym is a smaller version of the one she co-owned with Gemma in Dublin, but it is no less vital. It has quickly become a place of community. A hub where people come not just to train their bodies but to rebuild their spirits.

Gemma had visited often in those early months, her presence was a reminder of how far they had both come. She was doing well in Dublin; thriving as a business partner and still working with survivors to help them find their footing. Erin often thinks of Gemma as the sister she's chosen—a bond that is forged in fire and is unbreakable.

As for her family in Tyrone, the silence from them has been deafening, though not unexpected. Erin has long accepted that they are a part of the past she can't fully reclaim.

She has made a choice not to seek them out, knowing that even if she finds them, it will likely only lead to heartbreak. Still, a part of her holds on to the hope that one day, they might track her down; that she might see their faces again.

But Erin has stopped letting that hope define her. She has Callum now, his steadfast love grounding her, and Gemma, who will always be her sister in spirit. And here in Gweedore, she has found something she never thought she would: a sense of belonging.

She and Callum have settled into a small cottage just outside the village. Its whitewashed walls and thatched roof nestle among the wild grasses of the Donegal landscape.

Their days are filled with simple joys—early morning walks along the beach, evenings spent in the local pub where Callum plays guitar and Erin laughs with neighbours who have become their friends.

Life isn't perfect—she still carries her scars, both visible and invisible—but it is hers. And for the first time, Erin truly believes in the possibility of happiness.

As she turns from the cliff's edge and makes her way back towards the village, she feels a deep sense of peace. Gweedore has given her a second chance, and she intends to honour that gift by building something meaningful.

The wind catches her hair as she walks, carrying with it the faint scent of salt and heather. Behind her, the ocean roars on, vast and unrelenting; a reminder of both the battles she has fought and the strength she has found to endure. Erin O'Connor—the Irish Invincible—has finally come home.